THE BARRACKS THIEF

and Selected Stories

TOBIAS WOLFF

BANTAM BOOKS

TORONTO • NEW YORK • LONDON • SYDNEY • AUCKLAND

FOR LAUDIE

THE BARRACKS THIEF AND SELECTED STORIES

A Bantam Book / published by arrangement with
The Ecco Press

PRINTING HISTORY

The Ecco Press edition of THE BARRACKS THIEF was published April
15, 1984. The selected stories were taken from IN THE GARDEN OF
THE NORTH AMERICAN MARTYRS which was published
October 15, 1981.

Grateful acknowledgment is made to the following publications in which
the contents of this publication first appeared: Antaeus and Granta
(England)—The Barracks Thief; Antaeus—"In the Garden of the
North American Martyrs"; Atlantic Monthly—"The Liar" and
"Smokers"; Encounter—"Wingfield"; TriQuarterly—"Hunters
in the Snow"; Willowsprings—"Poaching."
Bantam edition / February 1986

The author wishes to thank the National Endowment for the Arts, the
Creative Writing Center at Stanford University, the Mary Roberts
Rinehart Foundation and the Arizona Council on the Arts and
Humanities for their generous support.

Windstone and accompanying logo of a stylized W are trademarks of
Bantam Books, Inc.

Library of Congress Cataloging in Publication Data

Wolff, Tobias, 1945-
  The barracks thief and other stories.

  Previously published as: The barrack thief. 1984.
  I. Title.
PS3573.0558B3   1984   813'.54   85-7400

ISBN 0-553-34213-4

Published simultaneously in the United States and Canada

PRINTED IN THE UNITED STATES OF AMERICA

SEM   0 9 8 7 6 5 4 3 2 1

Contents

THE BARRACKS THIEF

THE BARRACKS THIEF AND SELECTED STORIES by Tobias Wolff
THE BELL JAR by Sylvia Plath
BODILY HARM by Margaret Atwood
CANCER WARD by Alexander I. Solzhenitsyn
THE CONFESSIONS OF NAT TURNER by William Styron
THE CRYING OF LOT 49 by Thomas Pynchon
DANCING GIRLS AND OTHER STORIES by Margaret Atwood
DELTA OF VENUS Erotica by Anais Nin
DISTURBANCES IN THE FIELD by Lynne Sharon Schwartz
THE DIVINERS by Margaret Laurence
THE DOG OF THE SOUTH by Charles Portis
THE EDITORS' CHOICE: NEW AMERICAN STORIES,
    George E. Murphy, Jr.—Editor
THE END OF THE ROAD by John Barth
THE FIRST CIRCLE by Alexander I. Solzhenitsyn
FISHER'S HORNPIPE by Todd McEwen
THE GOLDEN NOTEBOOK by Doris Lessing
GOODBYE, COLUMBUS by Philip Roth
GRAVITY'S RAINBOW by Thomas Pynchon
THE HEADMASTER'S PAPERS by Richard A. Hawley
HOUSEKEEPING by Marilynne Robinson
HUNGER OF MEMORY by Richard Rodriguez
JOHNNY GOT HIS GUN by Dalton Trumbo
THE KILLING GROUND by Mary Lee Settle
LITTLE BIRDS by Anais Nin
THE LONG MARCH by William Styron
LOVE MEDICINE by Louise Erdrich
ONE DAY IN THE LIFE OF IVAN DENISOVICH
    by Alexander I. Solzhenitsyn
PITCH DARK by Renata Adler
THE RIVER WHY by David James Duncan
SET THIS HOUSE ON FIRE by William Styron
SLOW LEARNER by Thomas Pynchon
THE SNOW LEOPARD by Peter Matthiessen
SOMETIMES A GREAT NOTION by Ken Kesey
THE SOT-WEED FACTOR by John Barth
A SPY IN THE HOUSE OF LOVE by Anais Nin
THE STONE ANGEL by Margaret Laurence
SUNDOG by Jim Harrison
THE TIGER IN THE TIGER PIT by Janette Turner Hospital
AN UNKNOWN WOMAN by Alice Koller
V. by Thomas Pynchon

The Barracks Thief

❦

ONE

When his boys were young, Guy Bishop formed the habit of stopping in their room each night on his way to bed. He would look down at them where they slept, and then he would sit in the rocking chair and listen to them breathe. He was a man who had always gone from one thing to another, place to place, job to job, and, even since his marriage, woman to woman. But when he sat in the dark between his two sleeping sons he felt no wish to move.

Sometimes, because it seemed unnatural, this peace he felt gave him fears. The worst fear he had was that by loving his children so much he was somehow endangering them, putting them in harm's way. At times he knew for a certainty that some evil was about to overtake them. As the boys grew older he had this fear less often, but it still came upon him from time to time. Then he tried to imagine what form the evil might take,

1

from which direction it might come. When he had these thoughts Guy Bishop would close his eyes, give his head a little shake, and turn his mind to some more pleasant subject.

He was seeing a woman off and on. They had good times together and that was all either of them wanted, at least in the beginning. Then they began to feel miserable when they were away from each other. They agreed to break it off, but couldn't. There were nights when Guy Bishop woke up weeping. At one point he considered killing himself, but the woman made him promise not to. When he couldn't hold out any longer he left his family and went to live with her.

This was in October. Keith, the younger of the boys, had just begun his freshman year in high school. Philip was a junior. Guy Bishop thought that they were old enough to accept this change and even to grow stronger from it, more realistic and adaptable. Most of the worry he felt was for his wife. He knew that the break-up of their marriage was going to cause her terrible suffering, and he did what he could to arrange things so that, except for his leaving, her life would not be disrupted. He signed the house over to her and each month he sent her most of his salary, holding back only what he needed to live on.

Philip did learn to get along without his father, mainly by despising him. His mother held up, too, better than Guy Bishop had expected. She caved in every couple of weeks or so, but most of the time she was cheerful in a determined way. Only Keith lost heart. He could not stop grieving. He cried easily, sometimes for no apparent reason. The two boys had been close; now, even in the act of comforting Keith, Philip looked at him from a distance. There was only a year and a half between them but it began to seem like five or six. One night, coming in from a party, he shook Keith awake with the idea of having a good talk, but after Keith woke up Philip went on shaking him and didn't say a word. One of the cats had been sleeping with Keith. She arched her back, stared wide-eyed at Philip, and jumped to the floor.

"You've got to do your part," Philip said.

Keith just looked at him.

"Damn you," Philip said. He pushed Keith back against the pillow. "Cry," he said. "Go ahead, cry." He really did hope that Keith would cry, because he wanted to hold him. But Keith shook his head. He turned his face to the wall. After that Keith kept his feelings to himself.

In February Guy Bishop lost his job at Boeing. He told everyone that the company was laying people off, but the opposite was true. This was 1965. President Johnson had turned the bombers loose on North Vietnam and Boeing had orders for more planes than they could build. They were bringing people in from all over, men from Lockheed and Convair, boys fresh out of college. It seemed that anyone could work at Boeing but Guy Bishop. Philip's mother called the wives of men who might know what the trouble was, but either they hadn't heard or they weren't saying.

Guy Bishop found another job but he didn't stay with it, and just before school let out Philip's mother put the house up for sale. She gave away all but one of her five cats and took a job as cashier in a movie theater downtown. It was the same work she'd been doing when Guy Bishop met her in 1945. The house sold within a month. A retired Coast Guard captain bought it. He drove by the house nearly every day with his wife and sometimes they parked in front with the engine running.

Philip's mother took an apartment in West Seattle. Philip worked as a camp counselor that summer, and while he was away she and Keith moved again, to Ballard. In the fall both boys enrolled at Ballard High. It was a big school, much bigger than the one where they'd gone before, and it was hard to meet people. Philip kept in touch with his old friends, but now that they weren't in school together they found little to talk about. When he went to parties with them he usually ended up sitting by himself in the living room, watching television or talking to some kid's parents while everyone else slow-danced in the rec room downstairs.

After one of these parties Philip and the boy who'd brought him sat in the boy's car and passed a paper cup full of vodka back and forth and talked about things they used to do. At some point in their conversation Philip realized that they weren't friends anymore. He felt restless and got out of the car. He stood there, looking at the darkened house across the street. He wanted to do something. He wished he was drunk.

"I've got to go," the other boy said. "My dad wants me in early tonight."

"Just a minute," Philip said. He picked up a rock, hefted it, then threw it at the house. A window broke. "One down," Philip said. He picked up another rock.

"Jesus," the other boy said. "What are you doing?"

"Breaking windows," Philip said. At that moment a light came on upstairs. He threw the rock but it missed and banged against the side of the house.

"I'm getting out of here," the other boy said. He started the car and Philip got back inside. He began to laugh as they drove away, though he knew there was nothing funny about what he'd done. The other boy stared straight ahead and said nothing. Philip could see that he was disgusted. "Wait a minute," Philip said, grabbing the sleeve of the Nehru jacket the other boy had on. "I don't believe it. Where did you get the Nehru jacket?" When the other boy didn't answer Philip said, "Don't tell me—it's your dad's. That's why your dad wants you home early. He likes to know where his Nehru jacket is."

When they got to Philip's apartment building they sat for a moment without talking. Finally Philip said, "I'm sorry," and put out his hand. But the other boy looked away.

Philip got out of the car. "I'll give you a call," he said, and when he got no response he added: "I was just kidding about the Nehru jacket. It must have looked really great about twenty years ago."

Philip had always wanted to go to Reed College, but by the time he finished high school that year his grades were so bad he was lucky to graduate at all. Reed sent him a form rejection letter and so did the University of Washington, his second choice. He went to work as a busboy in a motel restaurant and tried to stay out of the apartment. Keith was always there, playing records or just lying around, his sadness plain to see though he had begun to affect a breezy manner of speech. Philip suspected that he was stoned a lot of the time, but he didn't know what to do about it, or if he should do anything at all. Though he felt sorry for Keith, Philip was beginning to dislike him. He wanted to avoid anything that might cause trouble between them and add to the dislike he felt. Besides, he had a smoke now and then himself. It made him feel interesting—witty, sensitive, perceptive.

Sometimes the owner of the theater where she worked gave Philip's mother a ride home. One night, coming home late himself, he saw them kissing in the owner's car. Philip turned around and went back up the street. The next day he refused to speak to her, and refused to tell her why, though he knew he was being theatrical and unfair. Finally it drove her to tears. As he sat reading Philip heard her cry out in the kitchen. He jumped up, thinking she must have burned herself. He found her leaning on the sink, her face in her hands. What had happened to them? Where were they? Where was her home, her cats, her garden? Where was the regard of her neighbors, the love of her family? Everything was gone.

Philip did his best to calm her. It wasn't easy, but after a time she agreed to go for a walk with him, and managed to collect herself. Philip knew he had been in the wrong. He told his mother that he was sorry, and that his moodiness had had nothing to do with her—he was just a little on edge. She squeezed his arm. This won't go on forever, Philip thought. In silence, they continued to walk the circular path around the small park. It was August and still warm, but the benches were empty. Now and then a pigeon landed with a rush of wings, looked around, and flew away again.

Their parish priest from the old neighborhood had friends among the local Jesuits. He succeeded in getting Philip a probationary acceptance to Seattle University. It was a good school, but Philip wanted to get away from home. In September he moved to Bremerton and enrolled at the junior college there. During the day he tried to keep awake in his classes and at night he worked at the Navy Yard, doing inventory in warehouses and dodging forklifts driven by incompetents.

Philip didn't get to know many people in Bremerton, but sometimes when he got off work at midnight he went drinking with a few of the Marine guards. Bremerton was a soft berth for them after a year in Vietnam. They'd been in the fighting, and some of them had been wounded. They were all a little crazy. Philip didn't understand their jokes, and if he laughed anyway they gave him mean looks. They talked about "asshole civilians" as if he weren't there.

The Marines tolerated Philip because he had a car, an old

Pontiac he'd bought for fifty dollars at a police auction. He ferried them to different bars and sometimes to parties, then back to the Yard through misty wet streets, trying to keep his eyes open while they laughed and yelled out the window and threw beer on each other. If one of them got into a fight all the others piled in immediately, no questions asked. Philip was often amazed at their brutishness, but there were times, after he'd let them off and watched them go through the gate together, when he envied them.

At Christmas Philip's mother asked him to talk to Keith. Keith was doing badly in school, and just before vacation one of his teachers had caught him smoking a joint in a broom closet. He'd been alone, which seemed grotesque to Philip. When he thought of Keith standing in the dark surrounded by brooms and cleanser and rolls of toilet paper, puffing away all by himself, he felt disgusted. Only by going down to the school and pleading with the principal, "groveling," as she put it, had Philip's mother been able to dissuade him from reporting Keith to the police. As it was, he'd been suspended for two weeks.

"I'll talk to him," Philip said, "but it won't do any good."

"It might," she said. "He looks up to you. Remember the way he used to follow you around?"

They were sitting in the living room. Philip's mother was smoking and had her feet on the coffee table. Her toenails were painted red. She caught Philip staring at them and looked down at her drink.

"My life isn't going anywhere," Philip said. He got up and walked over to the window. "I'm going to enlist," he said. This was an idea he'd had for some time now, but hearing himself put it in words surprised him and gave him a faint sensation of fear.

His mother sat forward. "Enlist? Why would you want to enlist?"

"In case you haven't heard," Philip said, "there's a war on." That sounded false to him and he could see it sounded false to his mother as well. "It's just something I want to do," he said. He shrugged.

His mother put her glass down. "When?"

"Pretty soon."

"Give me a year," she said. She stood and came over to Philip. "Give me six months, anyway. Try to understand. This thing with Keith has got me coming and going."

"Keith," Philip said. He shook his head. Finally he agreed to wait the six months.

They spent Christmas Day in the apartment. Philip gave Keith a puzzle that he worked on all afternoon and never came close to solving, though it looked simple enough to Philip. They had dinner in a restaurant and after they got back Keith went at the puzzle again, still with no success. Philip wanted to help, but whenever he offered a suggestion Keith went on as if he hadn't heard. Philip watched him, impatiently at first, then thoughtfully; he wondered what it was in Keith that found satisfaction in losing. If he went on the way he was, losing would become a habit, and he would never be able to pull his weight.

They had their talk but it went badly, as Philip knew it would. Though he tried to be gentle, he ended up calling Keith a coward. Keith laughed and made sarcastic remarks about Philip going into the service. He had suddenly decided that he was against the war. Philip pointed out that it had taken Keith seven tries to pass his driver's license examination, and said that anyone who had that much trouble driving a car, or solving a simple puzzle, had no right to an opinion on any subject.

"That's it," Philip told his mother afterward. "Never again."

A few nights later Philip came back from a movie and found his mother in tears and Keith trying to soothe her, though it was obvious that he was close to the breaking point himself. Oh, hell, Philip thought, but it wasn't what he had assumed. They weren't just feeling sorry for themselves. Philip's father had come by and when they refused to open the door for him he had tried to break in. He'd made a scene, yelling at them and ramming the door with his shoulder.

Philip left Keith with his mother and drove out to his father's place in Bellevue, an efficiency apartment near the lake. Guy Bishop had moved to Bellevue a few months earlier when the woman he'd been living with went to Sarasota to visit her family, and decided to stay there.

He still had his windbreaker on when he opened the door. "Philip," he said. "Come in." Philip shook his head. "Please, son," his father said, "come in."

They sat at a counter that divided the kitchen from the rest of the room. There were several pairs of gleaming shoes lined up along the wall, and the air smelled of shoe polish. On the coffee table there was a family portrait taken at Mount Rushmore in 1963. Keith and Philip were in the middle, grinning because the photographer, a Canadian, had just said "aboot" for "about." The four presidents, eyes blank, seemed to be looking down at them. Next to the picture a stack of magazines had been arranged in a fan, so that a strip of each cover was visible.

Philip told his father to stay away from the apartment. That was where the family lived, Philip said, and Guy Bishop wasn't part of the family.

Suddenly his father reached out and put his hand on Philip's cheek. Philip stared down at the counter. A moment later his father took his hand away. Of course, he said. He would call first thing in the morning and apologize.

"Forget the apology," Philip said. "Just leave her alone, period."

"It's not that simple," his father said. "She called me first."

"What do you mean, she called you first?"

"She asked me to come over," he said. "When I got there she wouldn't let me in. Which is no excuse for acting the way I did." He folded his hands and looked down at them.

"I don't believe you," Philip said.

His father shrugged. A moment later he looked over at Philip and smiled. "I've got something for you. It was meant to be a graduation present, but I didn't have a chance to give it to you then." He went over to the closet and pulled out a suitcase. "Come on," he said.

Philip followed him out of the room and down the steps into the parking lot. It had rained. The pavement shone under the lights, and the cars gleamed. Philip's father bent down and unzipped the suitcase. It was full of what looked like silver pipes. He lifted them out all at once, and Philip saw that they were connected. His father arranged them, tightening wing-nuts here and there, until finally a frame took shape with prongs at each end. He got two wheels from the suitcase and fastened them between the prongs. Then he bolted a leather seat to the top of the frame. It was a bicycle, a folding bicycle. He put down the kick-stand and stepped back.

"*Voilà*," he said.

They looked at it.

"It works," he said. He put up the kick-stand and straddled it, searching with his feet for the pedals. He pushed himself around the parking lot, bumping into cars, wobbling badly. With its little wheels and elevated seat the bicycle looked like the kind bears ride in circuses. The chrome frame glittered. The spokes caught the light as they went around and around.

"You'll never be without transportation," Philip's father said. "You can keep it in the trunk of your car. Then, if something breaks down or you run out of gas, you won't be forced to hitchhike." He almost fell taking a turn but managed to right himself. "Or say you go to Europe. What better way," he said, and then the bicycle caught the fender of a car and he pitched over the handlebars. He fell heavily. The bicycle came down with him and he lay there, all tangled up in it.

"My God," he said. "Give me a hand, son." When Philip didn't come to him he said, "I can't move. Give me a hand."

Philip turned and walked toward his car.

The next morning Philip got up early and took a bus downtown. The Marine recruiting office was closed. He wandered around, and when it still hadn't opened two hours later he walked up the street and enlisted in the Army. That night, when he knew his mother would be at work, he called home from Fort Lewis. At first Keith thought he was joking. Then the idea took hold. "You're really in the Army," he said. "What a trip. Jesus. Well, good luck. I mean that."

Philip could tell he was serious. It touched him, and he did something he came to regret. He gave Keith his car.

TWO

Five months later Keith disappeared. I was in jump school at Fort Benning when it happened, at the tail end of a training course that proved harder than anything I had ever done.

When I got the message to call home we had just come back from our third of five parachute jumps. We'd been dropped after a heavy rain and landed in mud to our ankles, struggling against a wind that pulled us down and dragged us through a mess of other men, scrub pine, tangled silk and rope. I was still spitting out mud when we got back to camp.

My mother told me that Keith had been gone for three days. He had left no message, not even a good-bye. The police had a description of the car and they'd talked to his friends, but so far they seemed no closer to finding him. We agreed that he had probably gone to San Francisco.

"No doubt about it," I said. "That's where all the losers are going now."

"Don't take that tone," she said. "It breaks my heart to hear you talk like that. Is that what you're learning in the Army?"

It had started to rain again. I was using an unsheltered pay phone near the orderly room, and the rain began to melt the caked mud on my uniform. Brown streams of it ran off my boots. "What do you want me to do?" I asked.

"I want you to go to San Francisco and look for Keith."

I couldn't help laughing. "Now how am I supposed to do that? This is Georgia, remember?"

"I've talked to a man at the Red Cross," she said. "You could get an emergency leave. They'll even lend you money."

"That's ridiculous," I said, though I realized what she was

saying was true. I could go on leave. But I didn't want to. It would mean missing the last two jumps, dropping out of the course. If I came back I would have to start all over again. I doubted I had the courage to do that; jump school was no day at the beach and I'd only made it this far out of ignorance of what lay ahead. I wanted those wings. I wanted them more than anything.

And if I did go, where would I look? Who would help me in San Francisco, me with my head shaved to the bone in a city full of freaks?

"You have to," she said. "He's your brother."

"I'm sorry," I told her. "It's just not possible."

"But he's so young. What is happening to us? Will somebody please tell me what is happening to us?"

I said that the police would find Keith, that he'd be glad to get home, that a taste of the real world would give him a new angle on things. I didn't believe what I was saying, but it calmed her down. Finally she let me go.

On our last jump, a night jump in full field equipment, a man was killed. His main chute didn't open. I heard him yell going down but it only lasted a moment and I paid no attention. Some clown was always yelling. It ended and there was no sound save the rhythmic creaking of my shoulder straps. I felt the air move past my face. The full moon lit up the silk above me, above the hundred other men falling in silence overhead and below and all around me. It seemed that every one of us fell under his own moon. Then a tree stabbed up to my right and I braced and hit the ground rolling.

The dead man was carried to the side of the road and left there for the ambulance. They didn't bother to cover him up. They wanted us to take a good look, and remember him, because he had screwed up. He had forgotten to pull his reserve parachute. As our truck went past him a sergeant said, "There's just two kinds of men in this business—the quick and the dead."

The fellow across from me laughed. So did several others. I didn't laugh, but I felt the impulse. The man lying by the road had been alive an hour ago, and now he was dead. Why did that make me want to smile? It seemed wrong. Someone was passing around a number. I took a hit and gave it to the man next to me. "All right!" he said. "Airborne!"

Two black guys started a jump song. I leaned back and looked up at the stars and after a while I joined in the song the others were singing.

THREE

After jump school I was sent to the 82nd Airborne Division at Fort Bragg. Most of the men in my company had served together in Vietnam. Like the Marines I'd known in Bremerton, they had no use for outsiders. I was an outsider to them. So were the other new men, Lewis and Hubbard. The three of us didn't exist for the rest of the company. For days at a time nobody spoke to me except to give me orders. Because we were the newest and lowest in rank we got picked to pull guard duty on the Fourth of July while everyone else scattered to Myrtle Beach and the air-conditioned bars in Fayetteville.

That's where I'd wanted to spend the Fourth, in a bar. There was one place in particular I liked. Smitty's. They had a go-go dancer at Smitty's who chewed gum while she danced. Prostitutes, Fayettecong we called them, gathered in the booths with pitchers of beer between them. Car salesmen from the lots down the street sat around figuring out ways to unload monster Bonnevilles on buck privates who made seventy-eight dollars a month before taxes. The bartender knew my name.

The last way I wanted to spend my Fourth was pulling guard with Lewis and Hubbard. We had arrived on the same day and avoided each other ever since. I could see that they were as lonely as I was, but we kept our distance; if we banded together we would always be new.

So when I saw the duty roster and found myself lumped together with them it made me bitter. Lewis and Hubbard were bitter, too. I could feel it in the way they looked at me when I joined them outside the orderly room. They didn't greet me, and while we waited for the duty officer they stared off in different directions. It was late afternoon but still steaming. The straight lines of the camp—files of barracks, flag-poles, even the white-washed rocks arranged in rows—wavered in the heat. Locusts sawed away in frantic bursts.

Lewis, gaunt and red-faced, began to whistle. Then he stopped. Our uniforms darkened with sweat. The oil on our rifles stank. Our faces glistened. The silence between us grew intense and I was glad when the first sergeant came up and began to shout at us.

He told us that we were little girls, piglets, warts. We were toads. We didn't belong in his army. He lined us up and inspected us. He said that we should be court-martialed for our ugliness and stupidity. Then he drove us to an ammunition dump in the middle of a pine forest thirty miles from the post and made us stand with our rifles over our heads while he gave us our orders and filled our clips with live rounds. We were to patrol the perimeter of the ammunition dump until he relieved us. He didn't say when that would be. If anyone so much as touched the fence we should shoot to kill. *Shoot to kill*, he repeated. No yakking. No grabass. If we screwed up he would personally bring grief upon us. "I know everything," he said, and he ordered us to run around the compound with our rifles still over our heads. When we got back he was gone, along with the three men whose places we had taken.

Lewis had the first shift. Hubbard and I sat in the shade of an old warehouse weathered down to bare gray boards with patches of green paint curling off. It had no windows. On the loading ramp where we sat two sliding doors were padlocked together and plastered with prohibitions, *No Smoking* and so on, with a few strange ones thrown in, like *No Hobnailed Boots*.

There were five other buildings, all in bad repair. Weeds grew between the buildings and alongside the chain-link fence. In places the weeds were waist-high. I don't know what kind of ammunition was inside the buildings.

Hubbard and I put our ponchos under our heads and tried to sleep. But we couldn't lie still. Gnats crawled up our noses. Mosquitoes hung in clouds around our heads. The air smelled like turpentine from the resin oozing out of the trees.

"I wish I was home," Hubbard said.

"Me too," I said. There didn't seem to be much point in ignoring Hubbard out here, where nobody could see me do it. But the word "home" meant nothing anymore. My father was in Southern California, looking for work. Keith was still missing. The last time I'd spoken to her my mother's voice had been cold, as if I were somehow to blame.

"If I was home," Hubbard said, "I'd be out at the drags with Vogel and Kirk. Don't ask me what I'm doing here because I sure don't know." He took off his helmet and wiped his face with his sleeve. He had a soft, square face with a little roll of flesh under his chin. It was the face he'd have for the rest of his life. "Look," he said. He took out his wallet and showed me a picture of a '49 Mercury.

"Nice," I said.

"It isn't mine." Hubbard looked at the picture and then put it away. "I was going to buy it before Uncle got me. I wouldn't race it, though. I'd take it out to the track and sit on the hood with Vogel and Kirk and drink beer."

Hubbard went on talking about Vogel and Kirk. Then he stopped and shook his head. "How about you?" he asked. "What would you be doing if you were home?"

"If I were home," I said, remembering us all together, "we would drive up to the fair at Mount Vernon. Then we'd have dinner at my grandfather's place—he has this big barbecue every year—and afterward we'd stay in a motel with a swimming pool. My brother and I would swim all night and watch the fireworks from the water."

We had not been to Mount Vernon since my grandfather

died when I was fourteen, so the memory was an old one. But it didn't feel old. It felt fresh and true, the starry night, the soft voices from the open doorways around the pool, the water so warm you forgot about it, forgot your own skin. Shaking hands with Keith underwater and looking up from the bottom of the pool at the rockets flaring overhead, the wrinkled surface of the water all ashimmer with their light. My father on the balcony above, leaning over the rail, calling down to us. That's enough, boys. Come in. It's late.

"You like it, don't you?" Hubbard asked.

"Like what?"

"All this stuff. Marching everywhere. Carrying a rifle. The Army."

"Come off it," I said. I shook my head.

"It's true," he said. "I can tell."

I shook my head again but made no further denials. Hubbard's admission that the car in the picture wasn't his had put me in an honest mood. And I was flattered that he had taken the trouble to come to a conclusion about me. Even this one. "The Army has its good points," I said.

"Name me one." Hubbard leaned against the ramp. He closed his eyes. I could hear Lewis whistling as he walked along the fence.

I couldn't explain why I liked the Army because I didn't understand the reason myself. "Travel," I said. "You can go all over the world."

Hubbard opened his eyes. "You know where I've been to? South Carolina, Georgia, and North Carolina. All I've seen is a lot of hicks. And when they do send us overseas it will just be to kill slopes. You know the first sergeant? They say he killed over twenty of them. I could never do that. I shot a squirrel once and cried all night."

We talked some more and Hubbard told me that he hadn't been drafted, as I'd assumed. Like me, he had enlisted. He said that the Army had tricked him. They'd sent a recruiter to his high school just before graduation to talk to the boys in Hubbard's class. The recruiter got them together in the gym and ran movies of soldiers being massaged by girls in Korea, and drinking beer in Germany out of steins. Then he visited the boys in their homes and showed each of them why the Army was the right choice. He told Hubbard that anyone who could drive a tractor automatically got to drive a tank, which turned out not to be true. Hubbard hadn't even set foot in a tank, not once. "Of course he didn't mention Vietnam," Hubbard said.

When I asked Hubbard what he was doing in the Airborne he shrugged. "I thought it might be interesting," he said. "I should have known better. Just more of the same. People running around yelling their heads off."

He waved his hand through the swarm of mosquitoes overhead. "We'll be getting orders pretty soon," he said. "Are you scared?"

I nodded. "A little. I don't think about it much."

"I think about it all the time. I just hope I don't get killed. They can shoot my dick off as long as they don't kill me."

I didn't know what to say. The sound of Lewis's whistling grew louder.

"Nuts," Hubbard said. "I don't know what he's so cheerful about."

Lewis came around the corner and climbed the ramp. "Shift's up," he said. "Best watch how you go along that fence. There's nettles poking through everyplace." He held out his hand for us to see. It was swollen and red. He leaned his rifle against the warehouse and began to unlace his boots.

"I'm allergic to nettles," Hubbard said. "I could die out there." He stood and put on his helmet. "Wish me luck. If I don't make it back tell Laura I love her."

Lewis watched Hubbard go, then turned to me. "I never saw so many bugs in my life," he said. "Wish I was at the beach. You ever been to Nag's Head? Those girls up there just go and go."

"Never been there," I said.

"I had one of those girls almost tore my back off," Lewis said. "Still got the marks." He leaned toward me and for a moment there I thought he was going to take his shirt off and show me his back as he'd shown me his hand.

"Ever been to Kentucky?" he asked.

I shook my head.

"That's where I'm from. Lawton. It's a dry town but I've been drinking since I was thirteen. Year after that I started on intercourse. Now it's got to where I can't go to sleep anymore unless I ate pussy."

"I'm from Washington," I said. "The state."

Lewis took off his helmet. He had close-cropped hair, red like his face. He could have worn it longer if he'd wanted, now that we were out of training. But he chose to wear it that way. It was his style.

He studied me. "You never been to Lawton," he said. "You ought to go. You won't want to leave and that's a guarantee." He took off one of his socks and started doing something to his foot. It seemed to require all his concentration. He sucked in his long cheeks and stuck the tip of his tongue out of the side of his mouth. "There," he said, and wiggled his toes. "I guess you know about what happened the other day," he said. "It wasn't the way you probably heard."

I didn't know what Lewis was talking about, but he gave me no chance to say so.

"I just didn't have the rope fixed right," he said. "I wasn't afraid. You ought to see me go off the high dive back home. I wanted to straighten out the rope was all."

Now I understood. Our company had practiced rappelling the week before off a fifty-foot cliff and someone had refused the descent. I'd heard the first sergeant raising hell but I was at the base of the cliff and couldn't make out what he was saying or see who he was yelling at.

"He called me Tinkerbell," Lewis said.

"He calls everybody that," I said. He did, too. Tinkerbell and Sweety Pie.

"You go ask around home," Lewis told me. "Just talk to those girls back there. They'll tell you if I'm a Tinkerbell."

"He didn't mean anything."

"I know what he meant," Lewis said, and gave me a fierce look. Then he put his sock back on and stared at it. "What's the matter with these fellows here, anyway? Pretty stuck on themselves if you ask me."

"I guess so," I said. "Look, don't mind me. I'm going to get some sleep before my shift." I closed my eyes. I hoped that Lewis would be quiet. He was starting to get on my nerves. It wasn't just his loud voice or the things he said. He seemed to want something from me.

"There's not one of these fellows would last a day in Lawton," he said. "We've got a guard in the bank that bit a man's tongue out of his head."

I opened my eyes. Lewis was watching me. "It's just because we're new," I said. "They'll be friendlier when we've been around for a while. Now if you don't mind I'm going to catch some sleep."

"What burns me," Lewis said, "is how you meet one of them in the PX or downtown somewhere and they look past you like they never saw you."

Off in the distance a siren wailed. The sound was weak, only a pulse in the air, but Lewis cocked his head at it. He squinted. When the siren stopped Lewis held his listening attitude for a moment, then gave a little shake. "I'm just as good as them," he said. "Look here. You got family?"

I nodded.

"I'm the only one left," Lewis said. "It was me and my dad, but now he's gone too. Heart attack." He shrugged. "That's all right. I get along just fine."

Another siren went off, right in my ear it seemed. The sound made me wince. Then everything went quiet. Lewis's eyes were pink.

Hubbard came around the side of the building and started up the ramp. I was glad to see him. He waved and I waved back. He gave me an odd stare then and I realized he'd only been flapping mosquitoes out of his face.

"There's a man out by the gate who wants to talk to us," he said.

Lewis started lacing up his boots. "Officer?"

Hubbard shook his head. "Civilian."

"What does he want?" I asked, but Hubbard had already turned away. I followed him and Lewis came after me, muttering to himself and trying to tie his boots.

There was a car parked in the turn-around outside the gate. It had a decal on the door and a red blinker flashing on top, dim in the gray light of early evening. A man was sitting in the front seat. Another man leaned against the fence. He was tall and stooped. He wiped at his face with a red bandana which he put in his back pocket when he saw us coming.

"Okay, mister," Hubbard said, "we're all here."

"Bet you'd rather be someplace else, too." He smiled at us. "Terrible way to spend the holiday."

None of us said anything.

The man stopped smiling. "We have a fire," he said. He pointed to the east, at a black cloud above the trees. "It's an annual event," the man said. "A couple of kids blew up a pipe full of matches. Almost took their hands off." He turned his head and barked twice. He might have been laughing or he might have been coughing.

"So what?" Lewis said.

The man looked at him, then at me. I noticed for the first time that his eyes were blinking steadily. "This isn't the best place to be," he said.

I knew what he meant—the dry weeds, the warped ramshackle buildings, the ammunition inside. "That fire's a mile off at least," I said. "Can't you put it out?"

"I think we can," he said. He tugged at his pants. It must have been a habit. They were already high on his waist, held there by leather suspenders. "The problem is," he said, "if you catch one spark in there that's all she wrote."

Hubbard and I looked at each other.

The man leaned against the fence. "You boys just come with us and I'll see that someone takes you back to Bragg."

"That's a good way to get dead," said Lewis. He cocked his rifle. The bolt slid forward with a sharp, heavy smack, a sound I'd heard thousands of times since joining the Army but never so distinctly. It changed everything. Everything became vivid, interesting.

The man froze. His eyes stopped their endless blinking.

"You heard me," Lewis said. "Let loose of that fence or you're dog meat."

The man stepped back. He stood with his arms at his sides and watched Lewis. I could hear the breath pass in and out of his mouth. A few minutes earlier I had been glad to see him. He was worried about me. He didn't want me to get blown up and that spoke well of him. But when I looked at him now, without weapon, without uniform, without anyone to back him up, I felt hard and cold. Nobody had the right to be that helpless.

None of us spoke. Finally the man turned and went back to the car.

"Godalmighty," Hubbard said. He turned to Lewis. "Why did you do that?"

"He touched the fence," Lewis said.

"You're crazy," Hubbard said. "You're really crazy."

"Maybe I am and maybe I'm not."

"You are," Hubbard said. "Take my word for it. Crazy hick."

"You calling me a hick?" Lewis said.

Out in the car I could see the two men talking. The one Lewis had scared off kept shaking his head.

"Tell me something, hick," Hubbard said. "Tell me what we're supposed to do if this place goes up."

"That's no concern of mine," Lewis said.

"Jesus," Hubbard said. He looked at me, appealing for help. I disappointed him. "What are you grinning at?" he said.

"Nothing," I said. But I might just as well have said "Everything." I liked this situation. It was interesting. It had a last-stand quality about it. But I didn't really believe that anything would happen, not to me. Getting hurt was just a choice some people made, like bad luck, or growing old.

"I don't believe this," Hubbard said.

"If you don't like it here," Lewis said, "you can go somewheres else. Won't nobody stop you."

Hubbard stared at the hand Lewis was shaking at him. It was beet-red and so bloated that you couldn't see his knuckles anymore. It looked like an enormous baby's hand, even to the crease around the wrist. "Godalmighty," Hubbard said. "Those must have been some killer nettles you ran into.

With plants like that I don't know what they need us for."

"Look," I said. "We've got a visitor."

The other man had gotten out of the car and was walking up to the fence. He smiled as he came toward us. "Hello there," he said. He took off his sunglasses as if to show us he had nothing to hide. His face was dark with soot. "I'm Deputy Chief Ellingboe," he said. He held up a card. When we didn't look at it he put it back in his shirt pocket. He glanced over at the man sitting in the car. "You certainly gave old Charlie there something to talk about," he said.

"Old Charlie about got his ears peeled," Lewis said.

"There's no call for that talk," the man said. He came up to the fence and looked at Lewis. Then he looked at me. Finally he turned to Hubbard and started talking to him as if they were alone. "I know you think you're doing your duty, following orders. I appreciate that. I was a soldier myself once." He leaned toward us, fingers wound through the iron mesh. "I was in Korea. Men dropped like flies all around me but at least they died in a good cause."

"Back off," Lewis said.

The man went on talking to Hubbard. "Nobody would expect you to stay in there," he said. "All you have to do is walk out and no one will say a thing. If they do I will personally take it up with General Paterson. Word of honor. I'll shake on it." He wiggled the fingers of his right hand.

"Back off," Lewis said again.

The man kept his eyes on Hubbard. He said, "You don't want to stay in there, do you?"

Hubbard looked over at Lewis. A fat bug flew between them with a whine. They both flinched. Then they smiled at each other. I was smiling too.

"You're a smart boy," the man said. "I can see that. Use the brains God gave you. Just put one foot in front of the other."

"You've been told to back off," Hubbard said. "You won't be told again."

"Boys, be reasonable."

Hubbard swung his rifle up and aimed it at the man's head. The motion was natural. The other man leaned out the car window and shouted, "Come on! Hell with 'em!" The deputy chief looked at him and back at us. He took his hands away from the fence. He was shaking all over. A grasshopper flew smack into his cheek and he threw up his arms as if he'd been shot. The car horn honked twice. He turned and walked to the car, got inside, and the two men drove away.

We stood at the fence and watched the car until it disappeared around a curve.

"It's no big deal," I said. "They'll put the fire out."

And so they did. But before that happened there was one bad moment when the wind shifted in our direction. We had our first taste of smoke then. The air was full of insects flying away from the fire, all kinds of insects, so many it looked like rain falling sideways. They rattled against the buildings and pinged into the fence.

Hubbard had a coughing fit. He sat on his helmet and put his head between his knees. Lewis went over to him and started pounding him on the back. Hubbard tried to wave Lewis off, but he kept at it. "A little smoke won't hurt you," Lewis said. Then Lewis began to cough. A few minutes later so did I. We couldn't stop. Whenever I took another breath it got worse. I ached from it, and began to feel dizzy. For the first time that day I was afraid. Then the wind changed again, and the smoke and the bugs went off in another direction. A few minutes later we were laughing.

The black smudge above the trees gradually disappeared. It was gone by the time the first sergeant pulled up to the gate.

He only spoke once on the drive home, to ask if we had anything to report. We shook our heads. He gave us a look, but didn't ask again. Night came on as we drove through the woods, headlights jumping ahead of us on the rough road. Tall pines crowded us on both sides. Overhead was a ribbon of dark blue. As we bounced through the potholes I steadied myself with my rifle, feeling like a commando returning from a suicide mission.

The first sergeant let us out at company headquarters. He said, "Sweet dreams, toads," and went off down the street, gunning the engine and doing racing-shifts on the gears.

We turned in our rifles and lingered outside the orderly room. We didn't want to go away from each other. Without saying so, we believed that we had done something that day, that we were proven men. We weren't, of course, but we thought we were and that was a sweet thing to believe for an hour or two. We had stood our ground together. We knew what we were made of now, and the stuff was good.

We sat on the steps of the orderly room, sometimes talking, mostly just sitting there. Hubbard suddenly threw his hands in the air. In a high voice he said, "Boys, be reasonable," and we all started laughing. I was in the middle. I didn't think about it, I just reached out and put my arms on their shoulders. We were in a state. Every time we stopped laughing one of us would giggle and set it off again. The yellow moon rose above the mess hall. Behind us the poker-wise desk clerk, "Chairborne" we called him, typed steadily away at some roster or report or maybe a letter to the girl he dreamed of—who, if he was lucky, kept a picture of him on her dresser, and looked at it sometimes.

FOUR

The three of us fooled around together for the next couple of days. One night we went to a movie in town, but Lewis spoiled it by talking all the time. You'd think he had never seen a movie before. If an airplane came on the screen he said "Airplane." If someone got hit he said "Ouch!" The next night we went bowling and he spoiled that, too. He had to use his left hand because his right hand was still swollen up, and his ball kept bouncing into the gutter. The people in the next lane thought it was funny, but it got on my nerves.

I was in a bad mood anyway. My mother had called the day after the Fourth to tell me that my car had been located in Bolinas, California. Two hippies were living in it. They said that Keith had sold it to them but they had no idea where he was now. They'd met him by chance in a crash pad in Berkeley. When my mother said "crash pad" I thought, Good God. I could see the whole thing.

She was beside herself. She said that she was going to quit her job and take a bus to San Francisco. Keith could be in trouble. He could be hungry. He could be sick. For a moment she didn't say anything, and I thought, He could be dead. I'm sure that's what she was thinking, too. I told her to stay home. When Keith got hungry he'd be in touch. There was no point in her wandering around a strange city, she'd never find him that way.

"Someone has to look for him," she said.

"Someone like me, you mean." I hadn't wanted to sound so rough. Before I had a chance to soften my words, though, my mother said, "How far away you are. Nothing reaches you."

We patched it up as well as we could. I told her I'd be

getting my orders for Vietnam any day now, and promised to look around for Keith while I was in Oakland waiting to ship out.

On Monday the rest of the company returned to duty. Almost everyone had been drinking all weekend, and looked it. Some of the men had been in fights. The ones who'd gone to the beach had terrible sunburns and were forced to walk stiff-legged because they couldn't bend their knees. As they marched they swayed from side to side like penguins. There were over thirty of them in this condition and when we moved out together it was something to see.

Two days later our company was detailed for crowd control. A group of protesters had camped out on the main entrance to the post, on either side of the road. We were supposed to keep them from moving past the gate.

At first it was friendly enough. The protesters waved and threw us sandwiches which we were forbidden to touch. Some of the women were good-looking in a soulful way and that didn't hurt their cause. The men were something else. They were all decked out in different costumes and seemed pleased with themselves in a way that I found disagreeable. There was one in particular I had my eye on. He was always chanting something, and he was the one who finally rounded everybody up and got them on the road.

They stood there for a while. With their arms joined they sang songs. Then they moved toward us. They stopped just short of the gate and began to talk to us. There was a tired-looking blond girl across from me and next to her was the fellow I'd been watching. I didn't care for him. He was prettier than the girl, and his long black hair curled up at the ends. He looked like Prince Valiant.

The girl said hello, and told me her first name. "What's yours?" she said.

I didn't answer. We'd been told not to, but I wouldn't have anyway.

Prince Valiant shook his head. "You're not allowed to talk," he said. "Doesn't that strike you as paradoxical? Here you are supposed to be defending freedom and you can't talk."

"Why do you want to kill your brothers?" the girl said.

The man next to me began swearing under his breath.

Prince Valiant smiled at him. "Speak up," he said loudly. "Haven't you ever heard of the First Amendment?"

The girl kept talking to me. "Your brothers and sisters in Vietnam don't want a war," she said. "If you didn't go, there wouldn't be any war."

"Don't be a C.I.A. robot," Prince Valiant said.

"Cocksucker," said the man next to me.

Prince Valiant smiled at him. He looked at me. "I think your friend's got a problem," he said.

I was trembling. I wanted to take my rifle to that smile of his and put it down his gullet. The sun was overhead, baking our helmets. Sweat ran down our faces. Everything got quiet. All along the line I could feel the tautness of something about to break. At that moment the highway patrol pulled up, four cars with lights flashing. The patrolmen got out and started clearing the protesters off the road. There was no resistance. Prince Valiant backed away. "You should get some help with that problem of yours," he said to the man beside me, who stepped forward out of line. The blond girl looked at us. "Please," she said, "please don't." She was pulling on Prince Valiant's arm. The first sergeant yelled at the man beside me to get back in line. He hesitated. Then he stepped back. Prince Valiant laughed and gave us the finger.

The protesters sang more songs, then broke up. After they left we were relieved by another company. I was still trembling. The other men were upset, too. We got back in time for dinner, but hardly any of us went to the mess hall. Instead we sat around and talked about what had happened, and what would have happened if they'd turned us loose. It was the first time I'd joined in a general conversation. While we were talking, Lewis came in. He'd been on KP that day so he'd missed the excitement. He listened for a while, then asked me in a loud voice if I wanted to go see the Bob Hope movie that was playing in town.

Everyone stopped talking.

I told Lewis no, I wasn't in the mood.

He looked at the other men. He stood there for a moment. Then he shrugged and walked outside again.

The stealing began a few days after the protest. A corporal had his wallet taken from under his pillow. It was found beneath the barracks steps, empty. The corporal swore that he'd had over a hundred dollars in it, which was probably a lie. Nobody in the company owned that much money except the clerk-typist, who regularly cleaned everyone out at marathon poker games in the mess hall.

Nothing like this had ever happened before in our company, not in anyone's memory, and everybody assumed that the thief must be from another unit—maybe even a civilian. Our platoon sergeants told us to keep our eyes open. That was all that was said about it.

The next night a man had his fatigue pants stolen while he slept. The thief balled them up and stuffed them into a trash can in the latrine along with his empty wallet. There was something intimate about this theft. Now we all knew, as these things are known, that the thief was one of us.

After the second theft our first sergeant went through all the barracks and made a speech. He had a vivid red scar that ran from the corner of one eye across his cheek and down under his collar. He had been badly wounded in Vietnam, so badly wounded that the Army was forcing him to take early retirement. He had just a few weeks left to go.

The scar gave weight to everything the first sergeant said. He spoke with painful slowness and agitation, as if each word was a fish he had to catch with his hands. He said that to his mind an infantry company was like a family, a family without any women in it, but a family. He wanted the thief to think about that, and then ask himself one question: What sort of a man would turn his back on his own kind?

"Think about it," the first sergeant said. Then he went to the barracks next door where through the open window we could hear him saying exactly the same thing.

Because the stealing was something new, and I was new, I felt accused by it. No one said anything, but I felt in my heart that I was suspected. It made me furious. For the first time in my life I was spoiling for a fight, just waiting for someone to say something so I could swing at him and prove my innocence. I noticed that Lewis carried himself the same way— swaggering and glaring at everyone all the time. He looked ridiculous, but I thought I understood. We were all breathing poison in and out. It was a bad time.

Hubbard was different. He seemed to wilt. He walked around with his hands in his pockets and his eyes on the ground, and I could hardly get a word out of him. Later I discovered that it wasn't the stealing that got him down, or the suspicion, but pure grief. His friends Vogel and Kirk had been killed, along with their dates, in a car smashup on the Fourth.

We all had our suspicions. My suspicions lay on a man who had never given me any reason to think badly of him. To me he just looked like a thief. I suppose that someone even suspected

Hubbard, miserable as he was. If so, Hubbard got clear of suspicion four days after the second theft.

It happened like this. He had left the mess hall early to take a shower. At some point he apparently looked up and saw someone lift his pants off the hook where he'd hung them. He shouted and whoever it was hauled off and hit him dead on the nose. He hadn't seen the thief's face because of the steam in the shower stall, and the blow knocked him down so he had no chance to give chase. His nose was broken, mashed flat against one cheek.

As soon as the story got around, the barracks emptied out. Everyone wanted to get away from the company that night. So did I. But I wanted to see Hubbard even more, partly out of concern and partly for some need that was not clear to me. So I sat on the orderly room steps and waited for him. Men from another company were playing softball on the parade ground. They yelled insults at each other until it got dark and they quit. Then I heard the smaller sounds, moths rustling against the bare light bulb overhead, frogs croaking, one of the Puerto Rican cooks in the mess hall singing happily to himself in that beautiful language that set him apart from us, and made him a figure of fun.

Hubbard came back from the hospital in a white jeep. He was wearing a shiny metal cast over his nose, held by two strips of tape that went across his face. The first sergeant met him and I waited while they talked. When Hubbard finally turned and started toward the barracks, I came up to him. We walked together without speaking for a moment, then I said, "Who was it?"

"I don't know," he said.

I followed him inside and sat on the next bunk while he took his boots off and stretched out, hands behind his head. He stared up at the ceiling. The cast gleamed dully.

"You really didn't see him?" I asked.

He shook his head.

"Well, I didn't do it," I said. "I swear I didn't." Without thinking about it I put my hand over my heart. I could feel my heart beating.

Hubbard looked at me. His lips were pressed together. He was utterly dejected. I could not imagine him pointing a rifle at someone's head. He looked back up at the ceiling. "Who said you did?" he asked.

"Nobody. I just wanted you to know."

"Fine," he said. "I never thought it was you anyway." Suddenly he turned his head and looked at me again. It made me uncomfortable.

"Just between us," I said, "who do you think it was?"

He shrugged. "I don't know. I'd like to be alone right now if that's all right with you."

"Whatever you want," I said. "If I can do anything, let me know. That's what friends are for."

At first he didn't answer. Then he said, "That was stupid, what we did out at the ammo dump. You probably think it was some big deal, but if you want to know the truth I almost throw up every time I think of it. We nearly got ourselves killed. Don't you ever think about that?"

"Sure I do."

"About being dead? Do you think about being dead?"

"Not exactly."

"Not exactly," he said. "Boy, you're really something. No wonder you like the Army so much."

I waited for Hubbard to go on, and when he didn't I stood up and looked down at him. His eyes were closed. "I'm sorry about what happened to you," I said. "That's why I came by."

"Thanks," he said, and touched the cast on his nose curiously, as if I had just reminded him of it. "It isn't only this," he said. Then, with his eyes still closed, he told me about his friends getting killed.

It spooked me. It was like a ghost story, the way Hubbard had talked about them so much on the day it happened. I thought I should say something. "That's tragic," I said, the word used in my family for all deaths, and as soon as it was out of my mouth I regretted it. I didn't know then that it is nearly impossible to talk to other people about their own suffering. Instead of giving up I tried again. "I know how you feel," I said. "I'd feel the same way if I lost my best friends."

"You don't have any," Hubbard said, "not like Vogel and Kirk, anyway." He rolled onto his side so that he was facing away from me. "Nobody that close," he said.

"How do you know?" I said.

"I just know."

I understood that Hubbard wanted me to leave. And I was glad to get away from him. It was too late to go anywhere so I went back to my own building. It was empty. I sat down on my bunk. I thought about what Hubbard had said, that I had nobody close. It got to me, coming from Hubbard, because we should have been close after what we'd been through together, he and Lewis and I.

Anyway, it just wasn't true.

I tried to read, but it took an effort in that big quiet room full of bunks. While I stared at the book I thought of other things. I wondered how I would hold up if I got wounded. I'd only been hurt once before, when I was eight, in a fall from a tree. My leg had been broken and I wasn't very brave about it. For several months everyone knew exactly how uncomfortable I was at any given moment. Keith was following me in those days. After I got out of the cast I walked with a limp, and Keith began to limp, too. It drove me crazy. I used to scream at him. Once I shot him with my B-B gun, trying to make him go away—but he kept limping after me, bawling his eyes out.

The door banged open and two men came in, a little drunk. Though it was still fairly early they turned off all the lights and went to bed. I had no choice but to do the same.

For a long while I lay in the dark with my eyes open. My unhappiness made me angry, and as I became more angry I began to brood about the thief. Who was he? What kind of person would do a thing like that?

FIVE

Lewis shuffles along the road leading out of Fort Bragg, muttering to himself and trying to hitch a ride, but he is so angry that he glares at all the drivers and they pass him up. He's angry because he couldn't talk his friends into going to the pictures with him. Bob Hope is his favorite actor but it's not as much fun going alone. He thinks they owed it to him to come.

When he gets to the bottom of Smoke Bomb Hill someone in a convertible stops for him. The driver of the convertible is a teacher who works at the elementary school on post. He is nervous, shy. Lewis leans over the side of the convertible and asks him something which he can't understand because Lewis's voice is so loud and thick. The teacher just keeps looking straight ahead and gives a little nod.

Lewis gets in. He tells the teacher that a fellow in Lawton had a car like this one and drove it across someone's yard one night and got his head cut off by a metal clothesline. They never did find the head, either. Lewis says he figures one of the dogs on the street got ahold of it and buried it somewhere.

He takes out a package of gum and crams four sticks in his mouth, dropping the wrappers on the floor of the car. He has unwrapped the last stick and is about to put it in his mouth when he remembers his manners and holds the gum out to the teacher. The teacher shakes his head, but Lewis stabs it at him until he takes it. When he starts to chew on it Lewis smiles and nods.

They leave the post and head toward town. The road is lined with drive-in restaurants and used-car lots advertising special deals for servicemen. American flags hang limp above the air-conditioned trailers where terms are struck, and sales-men in white shirts stand around in groups. In the early dusk their shirts seem to glow. The air smells of burgers.

The teacher sneaks a look at Lewis. Lewis says something incomprehensible and the teacher looks away quickly and nods. Lewis turns the radio on full blast and starts punching the buttons. When he doesn't get anything he wants he spins the tuning knob back and forth. Finally he settles on a tele-phone call-in show. People are calling in their opinions as to whether we should drop an atomic bomb on North Vietnam.

A man says we should, right away. Then a woman gets on the line and says that she believes the average person in North Vietnam is probably a lot like the average person here at home, and that their leaders are the ones making the trouble. She thinks we should be patient, and if that doesn't work then we should figure out a way to just bomb the leaders. Lewis chews up a storm. He watches the radio as if listening with his eyes.

He reminds the teacher of one of his students. It's the un-finished face, the way he stares, his restlessness. He asks Lewis to turn down the radio, and as Lewis reaches for the knob the teacher notices his hand—puffed-up and livid. In the five days since Lewis's brush with the nettles the swelling has hardly gone down at all. The teacher asks Lewis what hap-pened to it.

Lewis holds it up in front of his face and turns it back and forth. Nettles, he says. Hurts like hell, too, and that's no lie.

What did you put on it? the teacher asks.

Nothing, Lewis says.

Nothing?

I'm in the Army, Lewis says.

The teacher is going to say that Lewis should go on sick call, but he decides that they've probably bullied him into thinking there's something wrong with that. His father was an Army

officer and he knows how they do things. He feels sorry for
Lewis, for being helpless and in the Army and having his hand
so hideously swollen. You really should put some calamine
lotion on it, he says.

Never heard of it, Lewis says.

It's what you do for nettles, the teacher says. It eases the
pain and makes the swelling go down.

I don't know, Lewis says. I just as soon wait and see. Every
time you go to the doctor it ends up they stick a needle in you.

You don't have to go to a doctor, the teacher says. You can
buy it in a drugstore. Lewis nods and looks off. The teacher
can tell that he has no intention of spending his money on
calamine lotion. He can almost see that hand throbbing away,
getting worse and worse, and the boy doing nothing about it.
Everybody uses it, he says. We've always got a bottle around.

The teacher is not inviting Lewis to his home. He just wants
him to comprehend that calamine lotion is no big undertaking.
But Lewis misunderstands. What the hell, he says, I'll try anything once. Long as I get to the pictures by eight.

The teacher turns to explain. But there's no way to do it
without sounding like he's backing out. Just before they reach
town he pulls off on a side street bordered with pines. Almost
immediately the sound of traffic dies. The nasal voice coming
out of the radio seems unbearably loud and stupid. It embar-
rasses the teacher to belong to a species that can think such
things. When he stops the car in front of the house he sits for a
moment, letting the silence calm him.

They go in through a redwood gate in the back. Lewis whistles when he sees the pool, a piano-shaped pool designed by
the teacher's father, who also designed the house. The house
has sliding doors everywhere with rice-paper panels. All the
drawers and cabinets have brass handles with Japanese ide-
ograms signifying "Long Life," "Good Luck," "Excellent

Health." The teacher's father was stationed in Japan after the war and fell in love with Japanese culture. There's even a rock garden in the front yard.

The house is empty. The teacher's mother is visiting friends in California. His father died two years ago. The teacher leads Lewis to the living room and tells him to sit down. The chairs are heavy and ornately carved. The arms are dragons and the legs are bearded old men with their arms raised to look like they're holding the seats up. Lewis hesitates, then lowers himself into the smallest chair as if that is the polite thing to do.

The teacher goes to the medicine cabinet and takes out the calamine lotion. He comes back to the living room, shaking the bottle. He gives the bottle to Lewis, but Lewis can't open it because of his bad hand, so the teacher takes it back and twists off the cap. He gives the bottle to Lewis again, then sees that Lewis doesn't know what to do with it. Here, the teacher says. Look. He sits in the chair across from Lewis. He pulls the chair close. He pours some lotion into his palm, then takes Lewis's hand by the wrist and starts to work it in, over the swollen, dimpled knuckles, between the thick fingers. Lewis's hand is unbelievably hot.

Hey! Lewis says. That feels fine. I wish I had some before.

The burning skin drinks up the lotion. The teacher shakes more out, directly onto the back of Lewis's wrist. Lewis leans back and closes his eyes. The room is cool, blue. A cardinal is singing outside, one of three birds the teacher can identify. He rubs the lotion into Lewis's hand, feeling the heat leave little by little, the motions of his own hand circular and rhythmic. After a time he forgets what he is doing. He forgets his stomach which always hurts, he forgets the children he teaches who seem bent on becoming brutes and slatterns, he forgets his hatred of the house and his fear of being anywhere else. He forgets his sense of being absolutely alone.

So does Lewis.

Then the room is silent and gray. The teacher has no idea when the bird stopped singing. He looks down where his hand and Lewis's are joined, fingers interlaced. For once Lewis is still. He breathes so peacefully and deeply that the teacher thinks he is asleep. Then he sees that Lewis's eyes are open. There is a thin gleam of light upon them.

The teacher unclasps his hand from Lewis's hand.

I have to admit that stuff is all right, Lewis says. I might just go and buy me a bottle.

The teacher screws the cap on and holds the bottle out. Here, he says. Keep it. Go on.

Lewis takes it. Thanks, he says.

The teacher stands and stretches. I guess we'd better go, he says. You don't want to miss that movie.

Lewis follows him out of the house. He stops for a moment by the pool, which the teacher walks past as if it isn't there. The moon is full. It looks like a big silver dish floating on the water. Lewis puts his hand in his pocket and jingles the change.

He and the teacher don't talk on the way to town. Lewis leans into the corner, one arm hanging over the car door and the other on top of the seat. He strokes the leather with just that tenderness his dog used to feel. In town the sidewalks are crowded. Recruits with shaved heads, as many as fifteen or twenty in a group, walk from bar to bar, pushing each other and laughing too loudly, the ones in the rear almost running to keep up. They fall silent when they come up to the clusters of prostitutes, but when they are well past they call things over their shoulders. Different groups shout at each other back and forth across the street. The lights are on over the bars, in the tattoo parlors and clothing stores, in the gadget shops that sell German helmets and Vietcong flags, Mexican throwing knives, lighters that look like pistols, exotic condoms, fire-works and dirty books. The lights flash on the hood of the convertible and along the sides of the cars they pass.

The teacher stops in front of the movie theater. He tells Lewis to be sure and use that lotion and Lewis promises he will. They wave to each other as the convertible pulls away.

The previews are just beginning. Lewis buys a jumbo pop-corn and a jumbo Coke and a Sugar Daddy. He sits down. A giant tarantula towers over a house. From inside a woman looks out and sees the hairy legs and screams. Lewis laughs. That's some spider, he says out loud. The previews end and the first cartoon begins, a Tom and Jerry. Every time the cat runs into a wall or sticks his tail into a light plug Lewis cracks up. Now and then he shouts advice to the mouse. The couple in front of him move across the aisle and down. The next car-toon is a Goofy. Tinkerbell does the credits, flying from one side of the screen to the other, bringing the names out of her sparkling wand.

Tinkerbell, Lewis says. When he hears the word his stom-ach clenches. He gets up and walks outside. He stands under the marquee for a moment, just breathing, then runs down the sidewalk in the direction the convertible went, pushing people out of his way without regard. He runs three, four, five blocks to where the downtown ends. His eyes burn from the sweat running into them and his shirt is soaked through. He takes the bottle of calamine lotion out of his pocket and throws it into the road. It shatters. I'm no Tinkerbell, he says. He watches the cars go by for a while, balling and unballing his fists, then turns and walks back into Fayetteville to find a girl.

It is too loud, too bright. One of the women on the street smiles at him but he keeps going. He has never paid for it and he's not about to start now. He's never had it free either, but he came really close once at Nag's Head and has almost managed to forget that he failed. He turns off Combat Alley and heads down a side street. The bars give out. It is quiet here. He passes the public library, a red brick building with white pillars and high windows going dark one by one. A woman holds the door as people leave, mostly old folks. Just before she locks up two girls come out, a fat one in toreador pants and another girl in shorts, her legs white as milk. They both light cigarettes and sit on the steps. Lewis walks to the corner and turns back up the street. He stops in front of the girls. This here the library? he says.

It's closed, the fat one says.

Is that a fact, Lewis says, without looking at her. He watches the one in shorts, who is staring at her own feet and doing the French inhale with her cigarette. He can't see her face very well except for her lips, which are so red they seem to be separate from the rest of her. Shoot, Lewis says, I wanted to get this book.

What book? the fat one asks.

Just a book, Lewis says. For college.

The two girls glance at each other. The one in shorts straightens up. She walks down the steps past Lewis and looks up the street, leaning forward and lifting up one of her long legs like a flamingo.

You're from the post, the fat one says.

Here comes Bo, says the one in shorts. Give me another weed.

Both girls light fresh cigarettes. A car pulls up in front of the library, a '57 Chevy full of boys. The girl in shorts sticks her head in the window. She backs away, holding a beer and laughing. The door opens. She gets in and the car peels off.

The fat girl says, She is so loose, and grinds out the cigarette under her shoe.

The car stops at the end of the block and comes back in

reverse, gears screaming. The door opens again and the fat girl gets in and the car pulls away.

Lewis walks the side streets. He meets no girls, but once, passing an apartment building, he looks in a window and sees a pretty blond woman in nothing but her panties and bra watching television. He is about to rap on the glass when a little boy comes into the room pulling a wooden train behind him and yelling his head off. The train is on its side. Without taking her eyes off the screen the woman puts the train on its wheels.

Lewis heads back to Combat Alley. There are still a couple of women on the street, but he doesn't know how to go up to them, or what they will expect him to say. And there are all these other people walking by. Finally he goes into The Drop Zone, a bar with a picture of a paratrooper painted on the window.

Most of the prostitutes in town are reasonable women. Their reasons are their own and they aren't charitable, but they aren't crazy either. Mainly they want to do something easier than what they were doing before, so they try this for a while until they find out how hard it is. Then they go back to waitressing, or their husbands, or the bottling plant. Sometimes they get caught in the life, though, and there's a time right after they know they're caught when some of them do go crazy.

Lewis picks out the crazy one in a bar filled with reasonable girls.

She is older than the others and not the best looking, and the trouble she's in shows plainly. She hasn't brushed her hair all day and her dark eyes are ringed with circles like bruises. She is sitting by herself at the bar. The ice has melted in her ginger ale, which she pushes back and forth and never picks up. In a few years she will be talking to herself.

Lewis doesn't even look at any of the others. He is going to do something bad and she is the one to do it with. He goes straight to her and sits on the stool next to her. He avoids the bartender's gaze because he is not sure that he has enough money to pay for liquor and women both. *Liquor and women* are the words that come to his mind. He is really going to do it. Tonight, with her. He swivels on his stool and says, You come from around here?

She can't believe her ears. She stares at him and he looks down. His face is in motion, jerking and creasing and knotting. You want something? she says.

Lewis looks at her and looks away.

Well? she says.

No, he says. I mean maybe I do.

Well do you or don't you?

I don't know, he says. I never paid for it before.

Then go beat your meat, she says, and turns her shoulder to him.

The calamine lotion has dried pink on Lewis's hand and is starting to flake off. He picks at it with a fingernail. How much? he says.

She turns on him. Her eyes are raking his face. What are you trying to pull? she says. You trying to get me jugged or something?

All I said—

I know what you said. Jesus Christ. She dips into her shiny white bag and pulls out a cigarette. She glances around, lights it, and blows smoke toward the ceiling. Drop dead, she says.

Lewis doesn't know what he's done wrong, but he will have a woman and this is the woman he will have. Hey, he says, you ever been to Kentucky?

Kentucky, she says to herself. She grabs her purse and gets off the stool and walks out of the bar. Lewis follows her. When they get outside she whips around on him. Damn you, she says. What do you want?

I want to go with you.

She looks up and down the street. People move past them and no one pays them any attention. You don't give a shit, she says. I get jugged it's all the same to you.

You asked me did I want anything, Lewis says. What are you all mad about?

She says, I had enough of you, and turns away down the sidewalk. Lewis follows her. After a while he catches up and they walk side by side. I'll show you a time, Lewis says. That's a guarantee.

She doesn't answer.

Right down the street from where Lewis threw the bottle of calamine there is a motel with separate little bungalows. She stops in front of the last one. Ten dollars, she says.

How about eight?

Damn you, she says.

It's all I got.

She looks at him for a while, then goes up the steps and unlocks the door and backs into the bungalow. Let's have it, she says, and holds out her hand.

But there are only six ones in Lewis's wallet. He had forgotten the popcorn and the Coke and the Sugar Daddy. He hands the money to her. That's six, he says. I'll give you the rest on payday.

Drop dead, she says, and starts to close the door.

Lewis says, Hey! He gets his foot in and pushes with his shoulder. Hey, he says, give me my money back. She pushes from the other side. Finally he hits the door with his whole weight and it gives. She backs away from him. He goes after her. Give me my money back, he says. Then he stops. Put that knife away, he says. I just want my six dollars is all.

She doesn't move. She holds the knife as a man would, not raised by her ear but in front of her chest. Her breathing is hoarse but steady, unhurried.

All right, Lewis says. Look here. You keep the six dollars and I'll bring the rest tomorrow. I'll meet you tomorrow, same place. Okay?

I don't care what you do, she says. Just get.

Tomorrow, he says. He backs out. When he's on the steps the door bangs shut and he hears the lock snap.

The next day Lewis steals the first wallet. It is not under a pillow as the owner later claims but lying on his bunk in plain sight. Lewis sees it on his way to lunch and doubles back when everyone is in the mess hall. It holds two one-dollar bills and some change. Lewis takes the money and tosses the wallet under the barracks steps. He is mad the whole time, mad at the corporal for leaving it out like that and for being so stuck on himself and never saying hello, mad at how little money there is, mad at not having any money of his own.

He doesn't think of borrowing a few dollars from his friends. He has never borrowed anything from anyone. To Lewis there is no difference between borrowing and begging. He even hates to ask questions.

Later, when he hears that the corporal is telling everyone he had a hundred dollars stolen, Lewis gets even madder. That evening at dinner he stares at the corporal openly but the corporal eats without looking up. On his way out of the mess hall Lewis deliberately bumps against the corporal's chair, hard. He stops at the door and looks back. The man is eating ice cream like nothing happened. It burns Lewis up.

It also burns him up the way everybody just automatically figures the wallet was stolen by an outsider. They are so high and mighty they think nobody in the company could ever do a thing like that. *I'm no outsider,* he thinks. He gets so worked up he can't sleep that night.

The next day Lewis is assigned to a detail at the post laundry, humping heavy bags across the washroom. The air swirls with acrid steam. Figures appear and vanish in the mist, never speaking. It is useless to try and talk over the whining and thumping of the big machines, but now and then someone shouts an order at someone else. Lewis takes one short break in the morning but gets so far behind that he never takes another. All day he thinks about the woman in Fayetteville, how she looks, how bad she is. Doing it for money and carrying a knife. He is sure that nobody he knows has ever had a woman pull a knife on him. He thinks of different people and pictures to himself how they would act if they found out. It makes him smile.

When he gets back to the company he takes a shower and lies down for a while to catch his breath. Everyone else is getting ready for dinner, joking around, snapping each other with towels. Lewis watches them. His eyes sting from the fumes he's been working in and he closes them for a moment, just for a rest, and when he opens them again the barracks is dark and filled with sleeping men.

Lewis sits up. He hasn't eaten since breakfast and feels hollow all through. Even his legs seem empty. He remembers the woman in town, but it's too late now and anyway he doesn't have the money to pay her with. He imagines her sitting at the bar, sliding her glass back and forth.

It starts to rain. The drops rattle on the tin roof. A flash of lightning flickers on the walls and the thunder follows a while after, a rumble like shingle turning in a wave, more a feeling than a sound. Lewis gets up and walks between the bunks until he finds a pair of fatigue pants lying on a footlocker. He picks them up and goes to the latrine and takes the money out of the wallet. A five-dollar bill. Then he stuffs the wallet and pants into the trash can and goes back to bed.

He thinks about the woman again. At first he was sorry that he didn't meet her when he said he would, but now he's glad. *I will teach her something.* She probably thought she had him and it's best she know right off the kind of man she is dealing with. The kind that will come around when he gets good and ready. If she says anything he will just give a little smile and say, Honey, that's how it is with me. You can take it or leave it.

He wonders what she thinks happened. Maybe she thinks she scared him off with that knife. *That's a good one*, he thinks, him afraid of some old knife like you'd buy at a church sale. Kitchen knife. He remembers it pointed at him with the dim light moving up and down the blade, worn and wavy-edged from too many sharpenings, and it's true that he feels no fear. None at all.

As he dresses in the morning Lewis looks over at the man he stole from. The man is sitting on his bunk and staring at the floor.

The whole company knows about it by breakfast. And this time they know it's not an outsider but one of their own. Lewis can tell. They eat quietly instead of yelling and stealing food from one another, and nobody really looks at anybody else. Except Lewis. He looks at everyone.

That night the first sergeant comes through and makes a speech. It's a lot of crap about how an infantry company is like a family blah blah blah. Lewis makes himself deaf and leaves for town as soon as it's over.

In town Lewis looks for the woman in the same bar. But she isn't there. He tries all the bars. Finally he walks down to the bungalow. The windows are dark. He listens at the door and hears nothing. A TV on a windowsill across the street makes laughing noises. He sits and waits.

He waits for two hours and more and then he sees her coming down the sidewalk with the tiniest little man he has ever seen. You could almost say he's a midget. She's walking fast, looking at the ground just in front of her, and when they get close he can hear her muttering and him huffing to keep up. Lewis comes down the steps to meet them. Hey, says the little man, what the heck's going on?

Beat it, Lewis says.

Okay, okay, the little man says, and heads back up the street.

The woman watches him go. She turns to Lewis. Who do you think you are? she says.

Lewis says, I brought you the rest of the money.

She moves up close. I remember you, she says. You get out of my way. Get!

Here's the money, Lewis says, and holds it out to her.

She takes it, looks at it, drops it on the ground and walks past him up the steps. Four dollars, she says. You think I'd go for four dollars? Get yourself a nigger.

Lewis picks it up. I already gave you six, he says. This here is the rest.

You got a receipt? she says, and sticks her key in the lock.

Lewis grabs her arm and squeezes it. She tries to jerk away but he holds on and closes her hand around the money. That makes ten, he says. He lets go of her arm.

She gives him a look and opens the door. He follows her inside. She turns on the overhead light, kicks her shoes across the room, and goes into the bathroom. He can hear her banging around in there as he sits on the bed and takes off his shoes and socks. Then he stands and strips to his underwear.

She comes out naked. She is heavy in the ankles and legs and walks flat-footed, but her breasts are small, girlish. She drops her eyes as she walks toward him and he smiles.

All right, she says, let's have a look. She yanks his underpants to his knees and grabs him between her thumb and forefinger and squints down while she rolls him back and forth. Looks okay, she says, and drops him. You won't do any harm with that little shooter. Come on. She goes to the bed and sits down. Come on, she says again, I got other fish to fry.

Lewis can't move.

Okay, softy, she says, and goes to her knees in front of Lewis.

No, Lewis says.

She ignores him.

No! Lewis says, and pushes her head back.

Christ, she says. Just my luck. A homo.

Lewis hits her. She sprawls back on the floor. They look at each other. She is breathing hard and so is Lewis, who stands with his fists in front of him like a boxer. She touches her forehead where he hit her. There's a white spot. Okay, she says. She gives a little smile and reaches her hand out.

Lewis pulls her up. She leans into him and runs her hands up and down his neck and back and legs, dragging her fingernails. She stands on his feet and pushes her hips against his. Then she rises up on her toes, Lewis nearly crying out from the pain of her weight, and she presses her teeth against his teeth and licks his mouth with her tongue. She kisses his face and whenever he goes to kiss her back she moves her mouth somewhere else, down his throat, his chest, his hips. She puts her arms around his knees and takes him in her mouth and a sound comes out of Lewis like he has never heard another human make. He puts his hands along her cheeks and closes his eyes.

When he is close to finishing he tries to think about something else. He thinks about close-order drill. They are marching in review, the whole company on parade. The files flick past like rows of corn. He looks for a familiar face but finds none. Then they are gone. He opens his eyes and pulls back.

The regular way, he says. In bed.

He wants to hold her. He wants to lie quiet with her a moment, but she straddles him. She lowers herself onto him and digs her fingers into his flanks so that he rises up into her. He tries to move his own way, but she governs him. She puts her mouth on his and bites him. His foot cramps.

Then she rolls over and wraps her legs around his back and slides her finger up inside him. He shouts and bucks to be free. She laughs and tightens around him. She holds her mouth against his ear and presses with her teeth and murmurs things. Lewis can't make out what she's saying. Then she arches and stiffens under him, holding him so tightly he can't move. Her eyes are open halfway. Only the whites show. Lewis feels himself lift and dip as she breathes. She is asleep.

She sleeps for hours. Nothing disturbs her, not the argument in the street, nor Lewis stroking her hair and saying things to her. Then he falls asleep too.

When he wakes, her eyes are open. She is watching him. Hey there, he says. He reaches out and touches her cheek. He says the same words he was saying before he dozed off. I love you, he says.

She pushes his hand away. You garbage, she says. She slides off the bed and finds her purse where she dropped it on the floor and takes out the knife. He gets up on the other side and stands there with the bed between them.

You talk to me like that, she says. You come here and mock

me. You're garbage. I won't be mocked by you, not by you. You're just the same as me.

Let me stay, he says.

Get out of here, she says. Get! Get! Get!

Lewis dresses. I'll come back later, he says. He goes to the door and she follows him part way. I'll be back, he says. I'll bring you money.

She waves the knife. You'll get this, she says.

It's three o'clock in the morning. The last bus to camp left hours ago so Lewis has to make the trip on foot. The only cars on the road are filled with drunks. They yell things as they drive by. Once a bottle goes whistling past him and breaks on the shoulder. Lewis keeps going, feet sliding in his big square shoes. He doesn't even turn his head.

Just outside the base there is a tunnel with a narrow walkway along the side. The beams from the headlights of the cars glance off the white tiles and fill the tunnel with light. Lewis steadies himself on the handrail as he walks. One of the drivers notices him and leans on his horn and then the other drivers honk too, all together. The blare of the horns builds up between the tiles. It goes on in Lewis's head long after he leaves the tunnel.

He gets back to camp just after dawn and lies on his bunk, waiting for reveille. The man in the next bunk whistles as he breathes. Lewis closes his eyes, but he doesn't sleep.

At reveille the men sit up and fumble their boots on, cigarettes dangling, eyes narrowed against the smoke. Lewis thinks that he was wrong about them, that they are an okay bunch of fellows, not really conceited, just careful who they make friends with. He can understand that. You never know with people. He thinks about what good friends they are to each other and how they held the line in Vietnam against all those slopes. He wishes he had gotten to know them better. He wishes he was not this way.

For the next three days he tries to find a wallet to steal. At night, when he is sure that everyone is asleep, he prowls between the bunks and pats the clothes left on footlockers. He skips meals and checks under pillows and mattresses. As the days pass and he finds nothing he gets reckless. Once, during breakfast, he tries to break into a wall locker where he saw a man put his camera, one of those expensive kind you look through the top of, worth something as pawn, but the lock won't give and the metal door booms like thunder every time Lewis hits it with his entrenching tool. He feels dumb but he keeps at it until he can see there's no point.

During dinner on the fourth night he searches through the barracks next to his. There is nothing. On his way back out he passes the latrine and hears the hiss of a shower. He stops at the door. In one of the stalls he sees a red back through the steam, and, just outside, a uniform hanging on a nail. The bulge of the wallet is clear.

Lewis comes in along the wall. The man in the shower is making odd noises and it takes Lewis a moment to realize that he is crying. Lewis slips the pants off the hook and takes out the wallet. He is putting the pants back when the man in the shower turns around. His pink face floats in the mist. Hey! he says. Lewis hits him and the man goes down without a sound.

Outside the barracks Lewis falls in with the first group of men leaving the mess hall. He heads toward the parade ground and when he gets there he climbs to the top bench in the reviewing stands. He looks over in the direction of the company. No one has followed him, but men are drifting into small groups. They know that something has happened.

Lewis rubs his hand. It is still a little swollen and now it hurts like crazy from the punch he threw. He felt strange doing that, surprised and helpless and sad, like a bystander. What else will he watch himself do? He opens and closes his fingers.

There is a breeze. Halyards spank against the metal flagpole as the rope swings out and back.

He sees right away from the military I.D. that the wallet is Hubbard's. Lewis knows that he and Hubbard had a feeling once between them. He doesn't feel it now and can't recall it exactly, but he wishes he had not hit him. If there'd been any choice he'd have chosen not to. He pockets the money, three fives and some change, and looks through the pictures. Hubbard and a man who looks just like him standing in waders with four dead fish on the ground in front of them, one big one and three just legal. Hubbard in a mortarboard hat with a tassel hanging down. A car. Another car. A girl who looks exactly like Hubbard if Hubbard had a pony tail. An old man on a tractor. A white house. A piece of yellow paper folded up.

Lewis unfolds the paper and reads, *Dear Son*. He looks away, then looks back.

Dear Son, I have some very bad news. I don't think there is any way to tell you but just to write what happened. It was three days ago, on the Fourth. Norm and Bobby went down to Monroe to watch the drag races there. They were double-dating with Ginny and Karen Schwartz. From what I understand they and some of the other kids did a little "celebrating" at the track. Tom saw them and said they were not really drunk but you know how your brother is. Let's just say he isn't very observant. Norm was driving when they left for home.

They don't know for sure what happened but just the

other side of Monroe the car went into a skid and hit a truck parked off the road. Norm and Bobby and Ginny were killed right away. Karen died in the hospital that night. She was unconscious the whole time.

Dear, I know I should have called you but I was afraid I wouldn't be able to talk. Tom and I and Julie and even your father have been crying like babies ever since it happened. The whole town has. Everyone you see is just miserable. It is the worst thing to ever happen here.

This is about all I can write. Call collect when you feel up to it. Dear, don't ever forget that each and every person on this earth is a beautiful gift of God. Remember that always and you will never go wrong. Your loving Mother.

Lewis sits in the stands and shakes his head because Hubbard's mother is so wrong. She doesn't know anything. He would like to know what she thinks when she hears what just happened to Hubbard. Hubbard probably won't tell her. But if she knew, and if she knew about the woman in town and all the things Lewis has done, then she would know something real and give different advice.

He throws the wallet into the shadows under the stands. He starts to drop the letter after it but it stays between his fingers and finally he folds it up again and puts it in his pocket. Then he walks out to the road and hitches a ride to town.

She is not in any of the bars. Lewis goes to the bungalow and shakes the door. You in there? he says. The window is dark and he hears nothing, but he feels her on the other side. Open up, he says. He slams his shoulder against the door and the lock gives and he stumbles inside. From the light coming in behind him he can see the dark shapes of her things on the floor. He waits, but nothing moves. He is alone.

Lewis closes the door and without turning on the light walks over to the bed. He sits down. Breathing the bad air in here makes him light-headed. His arms ache from stacking oil drums all day in the motor pool. He's tired. After a time he takes off his shoes and stretches out on the twisted sheets. He knows that he has to keep his eyes open, that he has to be awake when she comes back. Then he knows that he won't be, and that it doesn't matter anyway.

It doesn't matter, he thinks. He starts to drift. The darkness he passes into is not sleep, but something else. *No*, he thinks. He pulls free of it and sits up. He thinks, *I have got to get out of here*.

Lewis can't tie his shoes, his hands are shaking so. With the laces dragging he walks outside and up the sidewalk toward town. He can hear everything, the trucks gearing down on the access road, the buzz of the streetlights, and from somewhere far away a steady, cold, tinkling noise like someone all alone breaking every plate in the house just to hear the sound. Lewis stops and closes his eyes. Dogs bark up and down the street, and as he listens he hears more and more of them. They're pitching in from every side of town. He wonders what they're so mad about, and decides that they're not really mad at all but just putting it on. It's something to do when they're all tied up. He lifts his face to the stars and howls.

The next morning Lewis wakes up feeling like a million dollars. He showers and shaves and puts on a fresh uniform with sharp creases. On his way to the mess hall he stands for a moment by the edge of the parade ground. They've got a

bunch of recruits out there crawling on their bellies and lob-
bing dummy hand grenades at truck tires. Sergeants are walking around screaming at them. Lewis grins.

At breakfast he eats two bowls of oatmeal and half a bowl of
strawberry jam. He whistles on his way back to the barracks.
Then the first sergeant calls a special formation and everything
goes wrong.

Lewis falls in with the rest of the company. He knows what
it's about. *Shoot*, he thinks. It doesn't seem fair. He's all ready
to make a new start and he wishes that everybody else could
do the same. Just wipe the slate clean and begin all over again.
There's no point to it, this anger and fuss, the first sergeant
walking up and down saying it gives him nerves to know there's
a barracks thief in his company. Lewis wishes he could tell him
not to worry, that it's all history now.

Then Hubbard goes to the front of the formation and Lewis
sees the metal cast on his nose. *Oh, Lord*, he thinks, *I didn't do
that*. He stares at the cast. There was a man in Lawton who
used to wear one just like it because his nose was gone, cut off
in a fight when he was young. Underneath was nothing but
two holes.

Hubbard follows the first sergeant up and down the ranks.
Lewis meets his eyes for a moment and then looks at the cast
again. *That hurts*, he thinks. He will make it up to Hubbard.
He will be Hubbard's friend, the best friend Hubbard ever
had. They'll go bowling together and downtown to the pictures. The next long weekend they'll hitch a ride to Nag's
Head and rustle up some of those girls down there. At night
they will go down on the beach and have a time. Light a fire
and get drunk and laugh. And when they get shipped overseas
they will stick together. They'll take care of each other and
bring each other back, and afterward, when they get out of the
Army, they will be friends forever.

The first sergeant is arguing with someone. Then Lewis sees that the men around him are emptying their pockets into their helmets and unblousing their boots. He does the same and straightens up. Hubbard and the first sergeant are in front of him again and Hubbard bends over the helmet and takes out the letter that Lewis could not let go of, that he's forgotten does not belong to him.

Where's my wallet? Hubbard says.

Lewis looks down.

The first sergeant says, Where is this boy's wallet?

Under the stands, Lewis says. While they wait Lewis looks at the ground. He sees the shadows of the men behind him, sees from the shadows that they are watching him. The first sergeant is saying something.

Look at him, the first sergeant says again. He puts his hand under Lewis's chin and forces it up until Lewis is face to face with Hubbard. Lewis sees that Hubbard isn't really mad after all. It is worse than that. Hubbard is looking at him as if he is something pitiful. Then Lewis knows that it will never be as it could have been with the two of them, nor with anyone else. Nothing will ever be the way it could have been. Whatever happens from now on, it will always be less.

Lewis knows this, but not as a thought. He knows it as a distracted, restless feeling like the feeling you have forgotten something when you are too far from home to go back for it.

The sun is hot on the back of his neck. A drop of sweat slides down between his shoulder blades, then another. They make him shiver. He stares over Hubbard's head, waiting for the next drop. Out on the parade ground the flag whips in a gust, but it makes no noise. Then it droops again. The metal cast glitters. Everything is still.

SIX

The morning after Hubbard got his nose broken the first sergeant called a special formation. He walked up and down in front of us until the silence became oppressive, and then he kept doing it. There were two spots of color like rouge on his cheeks. The line of his scar was bright red. I couldn't look at him. Instead I kept my eyes on the man in front of me, on the back of his neck, which was pocked with tiny craters. Finally the first sergeant began to talk in a voice that was almost a whisper. It was that soft, but I could hear each word as if he were speaking just to me.

He said that a barracks thief was the lowest thing there was. A barracks thief had turned his back on his own kind. He went on like that.

Then the first sergeant called Hubbard in front of the formation. With the metal cast and the tape across his cheeks, Hubbard's face looked like a mask. The first sergeant said something to him, and the two of them began to walk up and down the ranks, staring every man full in the face. I tasted something sour at the root of my tongue. I wondered how I should look. I wanted to glance around and see the faces of the other men but I was afraid to move my head. I decided to look offended. But not too offended. I didn't want them to think that this was anything important to me.

I composed my face and waited. It seemed to me that I was weaving on my feet, in tiny circles, and I made myself go rigid. All around me I felt the stillness of the other men.

Hubbard walked by first. He barely turned his head, but the first sergeant looked at me. His eyes were dark and thoughtful. Then he moved on, and I slowly let out the breath

I'd been holding in. A jet moved across the sky in perfect silence, contrails billowing like plumes. The man next to me sighed deeply.

After they had inspected the company the first sergeant ordered us to take off our helmets and put them between our feet, open end up. Then he told us to empty our pockets into our helmets and leave the pockets hanging out. My squad leader, an old corporal with a purple nose, said "Bullshit!" and put his helmet back on.

He and the first sergeant looked at each other. "Do it," the first sergeant said.

The corporal shook his head. "You don't have the right."

The first sergeant said, "Do it. Now."

"I never saw this before in my whole life," the corporal said, but he took his helmet off and emptied his pockets into it.

"Unblouse your pants," the first sergeant said.

We took our pantlegs out of our boots and let them hang loose. Here and there I heard metal hitting the ground, knives I suppose.

The first sergeant watched us. He had gotten his wounds during an all-night battle near Kontum in which his company had almost been overrun. I think of that and then I think of what he saw when he looked at us, bareheaded, our pockets hanging down like little white flags, open helmets at our feet. A company of beggars. Nothing worth dying for. He was clearly as disappointed as a man can be.

He looked us over. Then he nodded at Hubbard and they started up the ranks again. A work detail from another company crossed the street to our left, singing the cadence, spades and rakes at shoulder arms. As they marched by they fell silent, as if they were passing a funeral. They must have guessed what was happening.

Hubbard looked into each helmet as they walked up the

ranks. I had a muscle jumping in my cheek. And then it end-ed. Hubbard stopped in front of Lewis and bent down and took a piece of paper from his helmet. He unfolded it and looked it over. Then he said, "Where's my wallet?"

Lewis did not answer. He was standing two ranks ahead of me and I could see from the angle of his neck that he was staring at Hubbard's boots.

"Where is this boy's wallet?" the first sergeant said.

"The parade ground," Lewis said. "Under the stands."

The first sergeant sent a man for the wallet. Nobody spoke or moved except Hubbard, who folded the paper again and put it in his pocket. All my veins opened up. I felt the rush of blood behind my eyes. I was innocent.

When the runner came back with the wallet Hubbard looked through it and put it away.

"You stole from this boy," the first sergeant said. "You look at him."

Lewis did not move.

"Look at him," the first sergeant said again. He pushed Lewis's chin up until Lewis was face to face with Hubbard. They stood that way for a time. Then from behind, I could see Lewis's fatigue jacket begin to ripple. He was shaking con-vulsively. Everyone watched him, those in the front rank half-turned around, those behind leaning out and craning their necks. Lewis gave a soft cry and covered his face with his hands. The sound kept coming through his fingers and he bent over suddenly as if he'd been punched in the belly.

The man behind me said, "Jesus Christ!"

Lewis staggered a little, still bent over, his feet doing a jig to stay under him. He crossed his arms over his chest and howled, leaning down until his head almost touched his knees. The howl ended and he straightened up, his arms still crossed. I could hear him wheezing.

Then he dropped his arms to his sides and arranged his feet and tried to come to attention again. He raised his head until he was looking at Hubbard, who still stood in front of him. Lewis began to make little whimpering noises. He took a step forward and a step back and then he shrieked in Hubbard's face, a haunted-house laugh that went on and on. Finally the first sergeant slapped him across the face—not hard, just a flick of the hand. Lewis went to his knees. He bent over until his forehead was on the ground. He flopped onto his side and drew his knees up almost to his chin and hugged them and rolled back and forth.

The first sergeant said, "Dismissed!"

Nobody moved.

"Dismissed!" he said again, and this time we broke ranks and drifted away, throwing looks back to where Hubbard and the first sergeant stood over Lewis, who hugged his knees and hooted up at them from the packed red earth.

For the rest of that day we did target duty at the rifle range, raising and lowering man-sized silhouettes while a battalion of recruits blazed away. The bullets zipped and whined over the pits where we huddled. By late afternoon it was clear that the targets had won. We boarded the trucks and drove back to the company in silence, swaying together over the bumps, thinking our own thoughts. For the men who'd been in Vietnam the whole thing must have been a little close to home, and it was a discouraging business for those of us who hadn't. It was discouraging for me, anyway, to find I had no taste for the sound of bullets passing over my head. And it gave me pause to see what bad shots those recruits were. After all, they belonged to the same army I belonged to.

Hubbard ate dinner by himself that night at a table in the

rear of the mess hall. Lewis never showed up at all. The rest of us talked about him. We decided that there was no excuse for what he'd done. If the clerk had busted him at poker, or if someone in his family was sick, if he'd been in true need he could have borrowed the money or gone to the company commander. There was a special kitty for things like that. When the mess sergeant's wife disappeared he'd borrowed over a hundred dollars to go home and look for her. The supply sergeant told us this. According to him, the mess sergeant never paid the money back, probably because he hadn't found his wife. Anyway, Lewis wouldn't have died from being broke, not with free clothes, a roof over his head, and three squares a day.

"I don't care what happened," someone said, "you don't turn on your friends."

"Amen," said the man across from me. Almost everyone had something to say that showed how puzzled and angry he was. I kept quiet, but I took what Lewis had done as a personal betrayal. I had myself thoroughly worked up about it.

Not everyone joined in. Several men kept to themselves and ate with their eyes on their food. When they looked up they made a point of not seeing the rest of us, and soon looked down again. They finished their meals and left early. The first sergeant was one of these. As he walked past us a man at my table shouted "Blanket party!" and we all laughed.

"I didn't hear that," the first sergeant said. Maybe he was telling us not to do it, or maybe he was telling us to go ahead. What he said made no difference, because we could all see that he didn't care what happened anymore. He was already in retirement. The power he let go passed into us and it was more than we could handle. That night we were loopy on it.

I went looking for Hubbard. A man in his platoon had seen him walking toward the parade ground, and I found him there, sitting in the stands. He nodded when he saw me, but he did not make me welcome. I sat down beside him. It was dusk. A damp, fitful breeze blew into our faces. I smelled rain in it.

"This is where he went through my wallet," Hubbard said. "It was down there." He pointed into the shadows below. "What I can't figure out is why he kept the letter. If he hadn't kept the letter he wouldn't have gotten caught. It doesn't make any sense."

"Well," I said, "Lewis isn't that smart."

"I've been trying to picture it," Hubbard said. "Did you ever play 'Picture It' when you were a kid?"

I shook my head.

"It was a game this teacher of ours used to make us play. We would close our eyes and picture some incident in history, like Washington crossing the Delaware, and describe what we were seeing to the whole class. The point was to see everything as if you were actually there, as if you were one of the people."

We sat there. Hubbard unbuttoned his fatigue jacket.

"I don't know," Hubbard said. "I just can't see Lewis doing it. He's not the type of person that would do it."

"He did it," I said.

"I know," Hubbard said. "I'm saying I can't *see* him do it, that's all. Can you?"

"I'm no good at games. The point is, he stole your wallet and busted your nose."

Hubbard nodded.

"Listen," I said. "There's a blanket party tonight."

"A blanket party?" He looked at me.

For a moment I thought Hubbard must be kidding. Everyone knew what a blanket party was. When you had a shirker or a guy who wouldn't take showers you got together and threw a blanket over his head and beat the bejesus out of him. I had never actually been in on one but I'd heard so much about them that I knew it was only a matter of time. Not every blanket party was the same. Some were rougher than others. I'd heard of people getting beat up for really stupid reasons, like playing classical music on their radios. But this time it was a different situation. We had a barracks thief.

I explained all this to Hubbard.

"Count me out," he said.

"You don't want to come?"

Hubbard shook his head. A dull point of light moved back and forth across the metal cast on his nose.

"Why not?"

"It's not my style," he said. "I didn't think it was yours, either."

"Look," I said. "Lewis is supposed to be your friend. So what does he do? He steals from you and punches you out and then laughs in your face. Right in front of everyone. Don't you care?"

"I guess I don't."

"Well, I do."

Hubbard didn't answer.

"Jesus," I said. "We were supposed to be friends." I stood up. "Do you know what I think?"

"I don't care what you think," Hubbard said. "You just think what everyone else thinks. Beat it, okay? Leave me alone."

I went back to the company and lay on my bunk until lights-out. The wind picked up even more. Then it began to rain, driving hard against the windows. The walls creaked. Distant voices grew near as the wind gusted, then faded away. There should have been a real storm but it blew over in just a few minutes, leaving the air hot and wet and still.

After the barracks went dark we got up and made our way to

the latrine, one by one. For all the tough talk I'd heard at dinner, in the end there were no more than eight or nine of us standing around in T-shirts and shorts. Nobody spoke. We were waiting for something to happen. One man had brought a flashlight. While we waited he goofed around with it, making rabbit silhouettes with his fingers, twirling it like a baton, sticking it in his mouth so that his cheeks turned red, and shining it in our eyes. In its light we all looked the same, like skulls. A man with a cigarette hanging out of his mouth boxed with his own shadow, which went all the way up the wall onto the ceiling so that it seemed to loom over him. He snaked his head from side to side and bounced from one foot to the other as he jabbed upward. Two other men joined him. Their dog tags jingled and I suddenly thought of home, of my mother's white Persian cat, belled for the sake of birds, jumping onto my bed in the morning with the same sound.

The man with the flashlight stuck it between his legs and did a bump and grind. Then he made a circle on the wall and moved his finger in and out of it. Someone made panting noises and said, "Hurt me! Hurt me!" A tall fellow told a dirty joke but nobody laughed. Then someone else told a joke, even dirtier. No one laughed at his, either, but he didn't care. He told another joke and then we started talking about various tortures. Someone said that in China there was a bamboo tree that grew a foot a day, and when the Chinese wanted to get something out of a person or just get even with him, they would tie him to a chair with a hole in the bottom and let the tree grow right through his body and out the top of his head. Then they would leave him there as an example.

Somebody said, "I wish we had us one of those trees."

No one made a sound. The flashlight was off and I could see nothing but the red tips of cigarettes trembling in the dark.

"Let's go," someone said.

We went up the stairs and down the aisle between the bunks. The men around us slept in silence. There was no sound but the slap of our bare feet on the floor. When we got to the end of the aisle the man with the flashlight turned it on and played the beam over Lewis's bunk. He was sitting up, watching us. He had taken off his shirt. In the glare his skin was pale and smooth-looking. The beam went up to his face and he stared into it without blinking. I thought that he was looking right at me, though he couldn't have been, not with the flashlight shining in his eyes. His cheeks were wet. His face was in turmoil. It was a face I'd never really seen before, full of humiliation and fear, and I have never stopped seeing it since. It is the same face I saw on the Vietnamese we interrogated, whose homes we searched and sometimes burned. It is the face that has become my brother's face through all the troubles of his life.

Lewis's eyes seemed huge. Unlike an animal's eyes, they did not glitter or fill with light. His face was purely human.

He sat without moving. I thought that those eyes were on me. I was sure that he knew me. When the blanket went over his head I was too confused to do anything. I did not join in, but I did not try to stop it, either. I didn't even leave, as one man did. I stayed where I was and watched them beat him.

SEVEN

Lewis went into the hospital the next morning. He had a broken rib and cuts on his face. There was an investigation. That is, the company commander walked through the barracks with the first sergeant and asked if anyone knew who'd given Lewis the beating. No one said anything, and that was the end of the investigation.

When Lewis got out of the hospital they sent him home with a dishonorable discharge. Nobody knew why he had done what he'd done, though of course there were rumors. None of them made sense to me. They all sounded too familiar—gambling debts, trouble with a woman, a sick relative too poor to pay doctor bills. The subject was discussed for a little while and then forgotten.

The first sergeant's retirement papers came through a month or so later. He had served twenty years but I doubt if he was even forty yet. I saw him the morning he left, loading up his car. He had on two-tone shoes from God knows where, a purple shirt with pockets on the sleeves, and a pair of shiny black pants that squeezed his thighs and were too short for him. I was in the orderly room at the time. The officer of the day stood beside me, looking out the window. "There goes a true soldier," he said. He blew into the cup of coffee he was holding. "It is a sorry thing," he went on, "to see a true soldier go back on civvy street before his time."

The desk clerk looked up at me and shook his head. None of us had much use for this particular officer, a second lieutenant who had just arrived in the company from jump school and went around talking like a character out of a war movie.

But the lieutenant meant what he said, and I thought he was right.

The first sergeant wiped his shoes with a handkerchief. He looked up and down the street, and though he must have seen us at the window he gave no sign. Then he got into his car and drove away.

All this happened years ago, in 1967.

My father worked at Convair in San Diego, went East for a while to Sikorsky, and finally came back to San Diego with a woman he had met during some kind of meditation and nutrition seminar at a summer camp for adults. They had a baby girl a few weeks after my own daughter was born. Now the two of them run a restaurant in La Jolla.

Keith came home while I was in Vietnam. He lived with my mother off and on for twelve years, and when she died he took a room in the apartment building where he works as a security guard. He's had worse jobs. The manager gave him a break on the rent. All the tenants know his name. They chat with him in the lobby when they come in late from parties, and they remember him generously at Christmas. I saw him dressed up in his uniform once, downtown, where there was no need for him to have it on.

Hubbard and I got our orders for Vietnam at the same time. We had a week's leave, after which we were to report to Oakland for processing. Hubbard didn't show up. Later I heard that he had crossed over to Canada. I never saw him again.

I never saw Lewis again, either, and of course I didn't expect to. In those days I believed what they'd told us about a dishonorable discharge—that it would be the end of you. When I thought of a dishonorable discharge I thought of a man in clothes too big for him standing outside bus terminals and sleeping in cafeterias, facedown on the table.

Now I know better. People get over things worse than that. And Lewis was too testy to be able to take anyone's word for it that he was finished. I imagine he came out of it all right, one way or the other. Sometimes, when I close my eyes, his face floats up to mine like the face in a pool when you bend to drink. Once I pictured him sitting on the steps of a duplex. A black dog lay next to him, head between its paws. The lawn on his side was bald and weedy and cluttered with toys. On the other side of the duplex the lawn was green, well-kept. A sprinkler whirled rapidly, sending out curved spokes of water. Lewis was looking at the rainbow that hung in the mist above the sprinkler. His fingers moved over the dog's smooth head and down its neck, barely touching the fur.

I hope that Lewis did all right. Still, he must remember more often than he'd like to that he was thrown out of the Army for being a thief. It must seem unbelievable that this happened to him, unbelievable and unfair. He didn't set out to become a thief. And Hubbard didn't set out to become a deserter. He may have had good reasons for deserting, perhaps he even had principles that left him no choice. Then again, maybe he was just too discouraged to do anything else; discouraged and unhappy and afraid. Whatever the cause of his desertion, it couldn't have been what he wanted.

I didn't set out to be what I am, either. I'm a conscientious man, a responsible man, maybe even what you'd call a good man—I hope so. But I'm also a careful man, addicted to comfort, with an eye for the safe course. My neighbors appreciate me because they know I will never give my lawn over to the cultivation of marijuana, or send my wife weeping to their doorsteps at three o'clock in the morning, or expect them to be my friends. I am content with my life most of the time. When I look ahead I see more of the same, and I'm grateful. I would never do what we did that day at the ammunition dump, threatening people with rifles, nearly getting ourselves blown to pieces for the hell of it.

But I have moments when I remember that day, and how it felt to be a reckless man with reckless friends. I think of Lewis before he was a thief and Hubbard before he was a deserter. And myself before I was a good neighbor. Three men with rifles. I think of a spark drifting up from that fire, glowing as the breeze pushes it toward the warehouses and the tall dry weeds, and the three crazy paratroopers inside the fence. They'd have heard the blast clear to Fort Bragg. They'd have seen the sky turn yellow and red and felt the earth shake. It would have been something.

Hunters in the Snow

Tub had been waiting for an hour in the falling snow. He paced the sidewalk to keep warm and stuck his head out over the curb whenever he saw lights approaching. One driver stopped for him but before Tub could wave the man on he saw the rifle on Tub's back and hit the gas. The tires spun on the ice.

The fall of snow thickened. Tub stood below the overhang of a building. Across the road the clouds whitened just above the rooftops, and the street lights went out. He shifted the rifle strap to his other shoulder. The whiteness seeped up the sky.

A truck slid around the corner, horn blaring, rear end sashaying. Tub moved to the sidewalk and held up his hand. The truck jumped the curb and kept coming, half on the street and half on the sidewalk. It wasn't slowing down at all. Tub stood for a moment, still holding up his hand, then jumped back. His rifle slipped off his shoulder and clattered on the ice, a sandwich fell out of his pocket. He ran for the steps of the building. Another sandwich and a package of cookies tumbled onto the new snow. He made the steps and looked back.

The truck had stopped several feet beyond where Tub had been standing. He picked up his sandwiches and his cookies and slung the rifle and went up to the driver's window. The driver was bent against the steering wheel, slapping his knees and drumming his feet on the floorboards. He looked like a cartoon of a person laughing, except that his eyes watched the man on the seat beside him. "You ought to see yourself," the driver said. "He looks just like a beach ball with a hat on, doesn't he? Doesn't he, Frank?"

The man beside him smiled and looked off.

"You almost ran me down," Tub said. "You could've killed me."

"Come on, Tub," said the man beside the driver. "Be mellow. Kenny was just messing around." He opened the door and slid over to the middle of the seat.

Tub took the bolt out of his rifle and climbed in beside him. "I waited an hour," he said. "If you meant ten o'clock why didn't you say ten o'clock?"

"Tub, you haven't done anything but complain since we got here," said the man in the middle. "If you want to piss and moan all day you might as well go home and bitch at your kids. Take your pick." When Tub didn't say anything he turned to the driver. "Okay, Kenny, let's hit the road."

Some juvenile delinquents had heaved a brick through the windshield on the driver's side, so the cold and snow tunneled right into the cab. The heater didn't work. They covered themselves with a couple of blankets Kenny had brought along and pulled down the muffs on their caps. Tub tried to keep his hands warm by rubbing them under the blanket but Frank made him stop.

They left Spokane and drove deep into the country, running along black lines of fences. The snow let up, but still there was no edge to the land where it met the sky. Nothing moved in the

chalky fields. The cold bleached their faces and made the stub-
ble stand out on their cheeks and along their upper lips. They
stopped twice for coffee before they got to the woods where
Kenny wanted to hunt.

Tub was for trying someplace different; two years in a row
they'd been up and down this land and hadn't seen a thing.
Frank didn't care one way or the other, he just wanted to get
out of the goddamned truck. "Feel that," Frank said, slamming
the door. He spread his feet and closed his eyes and leaned his
head way back and breathed deeply. "Tune in on that energy."

"Another thing," Kenny said. "This is open land. Most of
the land around here is posted."

"I'm cold," Tub said.

Frank breathed out. "Stop bitching, Tub. Get centered."

"I wasn't bitching."

"Centered," Kenny said. "Next thing you'll be wearing a
nightgown, Frank. Selling flowers out at the airport."

"Kenny," Frank said, "you talk too much."

"Okay," Kenny said. "I won't say a word. Like I won't say
anything about a certain babysitter."

"What babysitter?" Tub asked.

"That's between us," Frank said, looking at Kenny. "That's
confidential. You keep your mouth shut."

Kenny laughed.

"You're asking for it," Frank said.

"Asking for what?"

"You'll see."

"Hey," Tub said, "are we hunting or what?"

They started off across the field. Tub had trouble getting
through the fences. Frank and Kenny could have helped him;
they could have lifted up on the top wire and stepped on the
bottom wire, but they didn't. They stood and watched him.

There were a lot of fences and Tub was puffing when they reached the woods.

They hunted for over two hours and saw no deer, no tracks, no sign. Finally they stopped by the creek to eat. Kenny had several slices of pizza and a couple of candy bars; Frank had a sandwich, an apple, two carrots, and a square of chocolate; Tub ate one hard-boiled egg and a stick of celery.

"You ask me how I want to die today," Kenny said, "I'll tell you burn me at the stake." He turned to Tub. "You still on that diet?" He winked at Frank.

"What do you think? You think I like hard-boiled eggs?"

"All I can say is, it's the first diet I ever heard of where you gained weight from it."

"Who said I gained weight?"

"Oh, pardon me. I take it back. You're just wasting away before my very eyes. Isn't he, Frank?"

Frank had his fingers fanned out, tips against the bark of the stump where he'd laid his food. His knuckles were hairy. He wore a heavy wedding band and on his right pinky another gold ring with a flat face and an "F" in what looked like diamonds. He turned the ring this way and that. "Tub," he said, "you haven't seen your own balls in ten years."

Kenny doubled over laughing. He took off his hat and slapped his leg with it.

"What am I supposed to do?" Tub said. "It's my glands."

They left the woods and hunted along the creek. Frank and Kenny worked one bank and Tub worked the other, moving upstream. The snow was light but the drifts were deep and hard to move through. Wherever Tub looked the surface was smooth, undisturbed, and after a time he lost interest. He stopped looking for tracks and just tried to keep up with Frank and Kenny on the other side. A moment came when he realized he hadn't seen them in a long time. The breeze was moving from him to them; when it stilled he could sometimes hear Kenny laughing but that was all. He quickened his pace, breasting hard into the drifts, fighting away the snow with his knees and elbows. He heard his heart and felt the flush on his face but he never once stopped.

Tub caught up with Frank and Kenny at a bend of the creek. They were standing on a log that stretched from their bank to his. Ice had backed up behind the log. Frozen reeds stuck out, barely nodding when the air moved.

"See anything?" Frank asked.

Tub shook his head.

There wasn't much daylight left and they decided to head back toward the road. Frank and Kenny crossed the log and they started downstream, using the trail Tub had broken. Before they had gone very far Kenny stopped. "Look at that," he said, and pointed to some tracks going from the creek back into the woods. Tub's footprints crossed right over them. There on the bank, plain as day, were several mounds of deer sign. "What do you think that is, Tub?" Kenny kicked at it. "Walnuts on vanilla icing?"

"I guess I didn't notice."

Kenny looked at Frank.

"I was lost."

"You were lost. Big deal."

They followed the tracks into the woods. The deer had gone over a fence half buried in drifting snow. A no hunting sign was nailed to the top of one of the posts. Frank laughed and said the son of a bitch could read. Kenny wanted to go after him but Frank said no way, the people out here didn't mess around. He thought maybe the farmer who owned the land would let them use it if they asked. Kenny wasn't so sure. Anyway, he figured that by the time they walked to the truck and drove up the road and doubled back it would be almost dark.

"Relax," Frank said. "You can't hurry nature. If we're meant to get that deer, we'll get it. If we're not, we won't."

They started back toward the truck. This part of the woods was mainly pine. The snow was shaded and had a glaze on it. It held up Kenny and Frank but Tub kept falling through. As he kicked forward, the edge of the crust bruised his shins. Kenny and Frank pulled ahead of him, to where he couldn't even hear their voices anymore. He sat down on a stump and wiped his face. He ate both the sandwiches and half the cookies, taking his own sweet time. It was dead quiet.

When Tub crossed the last fence into the road the truck started moving. Tub had to run for it and just managed to grab hold of the tailgate and hoist himself into the bed. He lay there, panting. Kenny looked out the rear window and grinned. Tub crawled into the lee of the cab to get out of the freezing wind. He pulled his earflaps low and pushed his chin into the collar of his coat. Someone rapped on the window but Tub would not turn around.

He and Frank waited outside while Kenny went into the farmhouse to ask permission. The house was old and paint was curling off the sides. The smoke streamed westward off the top of the chimney, fanning away into a thin gray plume. Above the ridge of the hills another ridge of blue clouds was rising.

"You've got a short memory," Tub said.

"What?" Frank said. He had been staring off.

"I used to stick up for you."

"Okay, so you used to stick up for me. What's eating you?"

"You shouldn't have just left me back there like that."

"You're a grown-up, Tub. You can take care of yourself. Anyway, if you think you're the only person with problems I can tell you that you're not."

"Is something bothering you, Frank?"

Frank kicked at a branch poking out of the snow. "Never mind," he said.

"What did Kenny mean about the babysitter?"

"Kenny talks too much," Frank said. "You just mind your own business."

Kenny came out of the farmhouse and gave the thumbs-up and they began walking back toward the woods. As they passed the barn a large black hound with a grizzled snout ran out and barked at them. Every time he barked he slid backward a bit, like a cannon recoiling. Kenny got down on all fours and snarled and barked back at him, and the dog slunk away into the barn, looking over his shoulder and peeing a little as he went.

"That's an old-timer," Frank said. "A real graybeard. Fifteen years if he's a day."

"Too old," Kenny said.

Past the barn they cut off through the fields. The land was unfenced and the crust was freezing up thick and they made good time. They kept to the edge of the field until they picked up the tracks again and followed them into the woods, farther and farther back toward the hills. The trees started to blur with the shadows and the wind rose and needled their faces with the crystals it swept off the glaze. Finally they lost the tracks.

Kenny swore and threw down his hat. "This is the worst day of hunting I ever had, bar none." He picked up his hat and brushed off the snow. "This will be the first season since I was fifteen I haven't got my deer."

"It isn't the deer," Frank said. "It's the hunting. There are all these forces out here and you just have to go with them."

"You go with them," Kenny said. "I came out here to get me a deer, not listen to a bunch of hippie bullshit. And if it hadn't been for dimples here I would have, too."

"That's enough," Frank said.

"And you—you're so busy thinking about that little jailbait of yours you wouldn't know a deer if you saw one."

"Drop dead," Frank said, and turned away.

Kenny and Tub followed him back across the fields. When they were coming up to the barn Kenny stopped and pointed. "I hate that post," he said. He raised his rifle and fired. It sounded like a dry branch cracking. The post splintered along its right side, up toward the top. "There," Kenny said. "It's dead."

"Knock it off," Frank said, walking ahead.

Kenny looked at Tub. He smiled. "I hate that tree," he said, and fired again. Tub hurried to catch up with Frank. He started to speak but just then the dog ran out of the barn and barked at them. "Easy, boy," Frank said.

"I hate that dog." Kenny was behind them.

"That's enough," Frank said. "You put that gun down."

Kenny fired. The bullet went in between the dog's eyes. He sank right down into the snow, his legs splayed out on each side, his yellow eyes open and staring. Except for the blood he looked like a small bearskin rug. The blood ran down the dog's muzzle into the snow.

They all looked at the dog lying there.

"What did he ever do to you?" Tub asked. "He was just barking."

Kenny turned to Tub. "I hate you."

Tub shot from the waist. Kenny jerked backward against the fence and buckled to his knees. He folded his hands across his stomach. "Look," he said. His hands were covered with blood. In the dusk his blood was more blue than red. It seemed to belong to the shadows. It didn't seem out of place. Kenny eased himself onto his back. He sighed several times, deeply. "You shot me," he said.

"I had to," Tub said. He knelt beside Kenny. "Oh God," he said. "Frank. Frank."

Frank hadn't moved since Kenny killed the dog.

"Frank!" Tub shouted.

"I was just kidding around," Kenny said. "It was a joke. Oh!" he said, and arched his back suddenly. "Oh!" he said again, and dug his heels into the snow and pushed himself along on his head for several feet. Then he stopped and lay there, rocking back and forth on his heels and head like a wrestler doing warm-up exercises.

Frank roused himself. "Kenny," he said. He bent down and put his gloved hand on Kenny's brow. "You shot him," he said to Tub.

"He made me," Tub said.

"No no no," Kenny said.

Tub was weeping from the eyes and nostrils. His whole face was wet. Frank closed his eyes, then looked down at Kenny again. "Where does it hurt?"

"Everywhere," Kenny said, "just everywhere."

"Oh God," Tub said.

"I mean where did it go in?" Frank said.

"Here." Kenny pointed at the wound in his stomach. It was welling slowly with blood.

"You're lucky," Frank said. "It's on the left side. It missed your appendix. If it had hit your appendix you'd really be in the soup." He turned and threw up onto the snow, holding his sides as if to keep warm.

"Are you all right?" Tub said.

"There's some aspirin in the truck," Kenny said.

"I'm all right," Frank said.

"We'd better call an ambulance," Tub said.

"Jesus," Frank said. "What are we going to say?"

"Exactly what happened," Tub said. "He was going to shoot me but I shot him first."

"No sir!" Kenny said. "I wasn't either!"

Frank patted Kenny on the arm. "Easy does it, partner." He stood. "Let's go."

Tub picked up Kenny's rifle as they walked down toward the farmhouse. "No sense leaving this around," he said. "Kenny might get ideas."

"I can tell you one thing," Frank said. "You've really done it this time. This definitely takes the cake."

They had to knock on the door twice before it was opened by a thin man with lank hair. The room behind him was filled with smoke. He squinted at them. "You get anything?" he asked.

"No," Frank said.

"I knew you wouldn't. That's what I told the other fellow."

"We've had an accident."

The man looked past Frank and Tub into the gloom. "Shoot your friend, did you?"

Frank nodded.

"I did," Tub said.

"I suppose you want to use the phone."

"If it's okay."

The man in the door looked behind him, then stepped back. Frank and Tub followed him into the house. There was a woman sitting by the stove in the middle of the room. The stove was smoking badly. She looked up and then down again at the child asleep in her lap. Her face was white and damp; strands of hair were pasted across her forehead. Tub warmed his hands over the stove while Frank went into the kitchen to call. The man who had let them in stood at the window, his hands in his pockets.

"My friend shot your dog," Tub said.

The man nodded without turning around. "I should have done it myself. I just couldn't."

"He loved that dog so much," the woman said. The child squirmed and she rocked it.

"You asked him to?" Tub said. "You asked him to shoot your dog?"

"He was old and sick. Couldn't chew his food anymore. I would have done it myself but I don't have a gun."

"You couldn't have anyway," the woman said. "Never in a million years."

The man shrugged.

Frank came out of the kitchen. "We'll have to take him ourselves. The nearest hospital is fifty miles from here and all their ambulances are out anyway."

The woman knew a shortcut but the directions were complicated and Tub had to write them down. The man told them where they could find some boards to carry Kenny on. He didn't have a flashlight but he said he would leave the porch light on.

It was dark outside. The clouds were low and heavy-looking and the wind blew in shrill gusts. There was a screen loose on the house and it banged slowly and then quickly as the wind rose again. They could hear it all the way to the barn. Frank went for the boards while Tub looked for Kenny, who was not where they had left him. Tub found him farther up the drive, lying on his stomach. "You okay?" Tub said.

"It hurts."

"Frank says it missed your appendix."

"I already had my appendix out."

"All right," Frank said, coming up to them. "We'll have you in a nice warm bed before you can say Jack Robinson." He put the two boards on Kenny's right side.

"Just as long as I don't have one of those male nurses," Kenny said.

"Ha ha," Frank said. "That's the spirit. Get ready, set, *over you go*," and he rolled Kenny onto the boards. Kenny screamed and kicked his legs in the air. When he quieted down Frank and Tub lifted the boards and carried him down the drive. Tub had the back end, and with the snow blowing into his face he had trouble with his footing. Also he was tired and the man inside had forgotten to turn the porch light on. Just past the house Tub slipped and threw out his hands to catch himself. The boards fell and Kenny tumbled out and rolled to the bottom of the drive, yelling all the way. He came to rest against the right front wheel of the truck.

"You fat moron," Frank said. "You aren't good for diddly."

Tub grabbed Frank by the collar and backed him hard up against the fence. Frank tried to pull his hands away but Tub shook him and snapped his head back and forth and finally Frank gave up.

"What do you know about fat," Tub said. "What do you know about glands." As he spoke he kept shaking Frank. "What do you know about me."

"All right," Frank said.

"No more," Tub said.

"All right."

"No more talking to me like that. No more watching. No more laughing."

"Okay, Tub. I promise."

Tub let go of Frank and leaned his forehead against the fence. His arms hung straight at his sides.

"I'm sorry, Tub." Frank touched him on the shoulder. "I'll be down at the truck."

Tub stood by the fence for a while and then got the rifles off the porch. Frank had rolled Kenny back onto the boards and they lifted him into the bed of the truck. Frank spread the seat blankets over him. "Warm enough?" he asked.

Kenny nodded.

"Okay. Now how does reverse work on this thing?"

"All the way to the left and up." Kenny sat up as Frank started forward to the cab. "Frank!"

"What?"

"If it sticks don't force it."

The truck started right away. "One thing," Frank said, "you've got to hand it to the Japanese. A very ancient, very spiritual culture and they can still make a hell of a truck." He glanced over at Tub. "Look, I'm sorry. I didn't know you felt that way, honest to God I didn't. You should have said something."

"I did."

"When? Name one time."

"A couple of hours ago."

"I guess I wasn't paying attention."

"That's true, Frank," Tub said. "You don't pay attention very much."

"Tub," Frank said, "what happened back there, I should have been more sympathetic. I realize that. You were going through a lot. I just want you to know it wasn't your fault. He was asking for it."

"You think so?"

"Absolutely. It was him or you. I would have done the same thing in your shoes, no question."

The wind was blowing into their faces. The snow was a

moving white wall in front of their lights; it swirled into the cab through the hole in the windshield and settled on them. Tub clapped his hands and shifted around to stay warm, but it didn't work.

"I'm going to have to stop," Frank said. "I can't feel my fingers."

Up ahead they saw some lights off the road. It was a tavern. Outside in the parking lot there were several jeeps and trucks. A couple of them had deer strapped across their hoods. Frank parked and they went back to Kenny. "How you doing, partner," Frank said.

"I'm cold."

"Well, don't feel like the Lone Ranger. It's worse inside, take my word for it. You should get that windshield fixed."

"Look," Tub said, "he threw the blankets off." They were lying in a heap against the tailgate.

"Now look, Kenny," Frank said, "it's no use whining about being cold if you're not going to try and keep warm. You've got to do your share." He spread the blankets over Kenny and tucked them in at the corners.

"They blew off."

"Hold on to them then."

"Why are we stopping, Frank?"

"Because if me and Tub don't get warmed up we're going to freeze solid and then where will you be?" He punched Kenny lightly in the arm. "So just hold your horses."

The bar was full of men in colored jackets, mostly orange. The waitress brought coffee. "Just what the doctor ordered," Frank said, cradling the steaming cup in his hand. His skin was bone white. "Tub, I've been thinking. What you said about me not paying attention, that's true."

"It's okay."

"No. I really had that coming. I guess I've just been a little too interested in old number one. I've had a lot on my mind. Not that that's any excuse."

"Forget it, Frank. I sort of lost my temper back there. I guess we're all a little on edge."

Frank shook his head. "It isn't just that."

"You want to talk about it?"

"Just between us, Tub?"

"Sure, Frank. Just between us."

"Tub, I think I'm going to be leaving Nancy."

"Oh, Frank. Oh, Frank." Tub sat back and shook his head.

Frank reached out and laid his hand on Tub's arm. "Tub, have you ever been really in love?"

"Well—"

"I mean *really* in love." He squeezed Tub's wrist. "With your whole being."

"I don't know. When you put it like that, I don't know."

"You haven't then. Nothing against you, but you'd know it if you had." Frank let go of Tub's arm. "This isn't just some bit of fluff I'm talking about."

"Who is she, Frank?"

Frank paused. He looked into his empty cup. "Roxanne Brewer."

"Cliff Brewer's kid? The babysitter?"

"You can't just put people into categories like that, Tub. That's why the whole system is wrong. And that's why this country is going to hell in a rowboat."

"But she can't be more than—" Tub shook his head.

"Fifteen. She'll be sixteen in May." Frank smiled. "May fourth, three twenty-seven p.m. Hell, Tub, a hundred years ago she'd have been an old maid by that age. Juliet was only thirteen."

"Juliet? Juliet Miller? Jesus, Frank, she doesn't even have breasts. She doesn't even wear a top to her bathing suit. She's still collecting frogs."

"Not Juliet Miller. The real Juliet. Tub, don't you see how you're dividing people up into categories? He's an executive, she's a secretary, he's a truck driver, she's fifteen years old. Tub, this so-called babysitter, this so-called fifteen-year-old has more in her little finger than most of us have in our entire bodies. I can tell you this little lady is something special."

Tub nodded. "I know the kids like her."

"She's opened up whole worlds to me that I never knew were there."

"What does Nancy think about all of this?"

"She doesn't know."

"You haven't told her?"

"Not yet. It's not so easy. She's been damned good to me all these years. Then there's the kids to consider." The brightness in Frank's eyes trembled and he wiped quickly at them with the back of his hand. "I guess you think I'm a complete bastard."

"No, Frank. I don't think that."

"Well, you *ought* to."

"Frank, when you've got a friend it means you've always got someone on your side, no matter what. That's the way I feel about it, anyway."

"You mean that, Tub?"

"Sure I do."

Frank smiled. "You don't know how good it feels to hear you say that."

Kenny had tried to get out of the truck but he hadn't made it. He was jackknifed over the tailgate, his head hanging above the bumper. They lifted him back into the bed and covered him again. He was sweating and his teeth chattered. "It hurts, Frank."

"It wouldn't hurt so much if you just stayed put. Now we're going to the hospital. Got that? Say it—I'm going to the hospital."

"I'm going to the hospital."

"Again."

"I'm going to the hospital."

"Now just keep saying that to yourself and before you know it we'll be there."

After they had gone a few miles Tub turned to Frank. "I just pulled a real boner," he said.

"What's that?"

"I left the directions on the table back there."

"That's okay. I remember them pretty well."

The snowfall lightened and the clouds began to roll back off the fields, but it was no warmer and after a time both Frank and Tub were bitten through and shaking. Frank almost didn't make it around a curve, and they decided to stop at the next roadhouse.

There was an automatic hand-dryer in the bathroom and they took turns standing in front of it, opening their jackets and shirts and letting the jet of hot air breathe across their faces and chests.

"You know," Tub said, "what you told me back there, I appreciate it. Trusting me."

Frank opened and closed his fingers in front of the nozzle. "The way I look at it, Tub, no man is an island. You've got to trust someone."

"Frank—"

Frank waited.

"When I said that about my glands, that wasn't true. The truth is I just shovel it in."

"Well, Tub—"

"Day and night, Frank. In the shower. On the freeway." He turned and let the air play over his back. "I've even got stuff in the paper towel machine at work."

"There's nothing wrong with your glands at all?" Frank had taken his boots and socks off. He held first his right, then his left foot up to the nozzle.

"No. There never was."

"Does Alice know?" The machine went off and Frank started lacing up his boots.

"Nobody knows. That's the worst of it, Frank. Not the being fat, I never got any big kick out of being thin, but the lying. Having to lead a double life like a spy or a hit man. This sounds strange but I feel sorry for those guys, I really do. I know what they go through. Always having to think about what you say and do. Always feeling like people are watching you, trying to catch you at something. Never able to just be yourself. Like when I make a big deal about only having an orange for breakfast and then scarf all the way to work. Oreos, Mars Bars, Twinkies. Sugar Babies. Snickers." Tub glanced at Frank and looked quickly away. "Pretty disgusting, isn't it?"

"Tub. Tub." Frank shook his head. "Come on." He took Tub's arm and led him into the restaurant half of the bar. "My friend is hungry," he told the waitress. "Bring four orders of pancakes, plenty of butter and syrup."

"Frank—"

"Sit down."

When the dishes came Frank carved out slabs of butter and just laid them on the pancakes. Then he emptied the bottle of syrup, moving it back and forth over the plates. He leaned forward on his elbows and rested his chin in one hand. "Go on, Tub."

Tub ate several mouthfuls, then started to wipe his lips. Frank took the napkin away from him. "No wiping," he said. Tub kept at it. The syrup covered his chin; it dripped to a point like a goatee. "Weigh in, Tub," Frank said, pushing another fork across the table. "Get down to business." Tub took the fork in his left hand and lowered his head and started really chowing down. "Clean your plate," Frank said when the pancakes were gone, and Tub lifted each of the four plates and licked it clean. He sat back, trying to catch his breath.

"Beautiful," Frank said. "Are you full?"

"I'm full," Tub said. "I've never been so full."

Kenny's blankets were bunched up against the tailgate again.

"They must have blown off," Tub said.

"They're not doing him any good," Frank said. "We might as well get some use out of them."

Kenny mumbled. Tub bent over him. "What? Speak up."

"I'm going to the hospital," Kenny said.

"Attaboy," Frank said.

The blankets helped. The wind still got their faces and Frank's hands but it was much better. The fresh snow on the road and the trees sparkled under the beam of the headlight. Squares of light from farmhouse windows fell onto the blue snow in the fields.

"Frank," Tub said after a time, "you know that farmer? He told Kenny to kill the dog."

"You're kidding!" Frank leaned forward, considering. "That Kenny. What a card." He laughed and so did Tub. Tub smiled out the back window. Kenny lay with his arms folded over his stomach, moving his lips at the stars. Right overhead was the Big Dipper, and behind, hanging between Kenny's toes in the direction of the hospital, was the North Star, Pole Star, Help to Sailors. As the truck twisted through the gentle hills the star went back and forth between Kenny's boots, staying always in his sight. "I'm going to the hospital," Kenny said. But he was wrong. They had taken a different turn a long way back.

Smokers

I noticed Eugene before I actually met him. There was no way not to notice him. As our train was leaving New York, Eugene, moving from another coach into the one where I sat, managed to get himself jammed in the door between his two enormous suitcases. I watched as he struggled to free himself, fascinated by the hat he wore, a green Alpine hat with feathers stuck in the brim. I wondered if he hoped to reduce the absurdity of his situation by grinning as he did in every direction. Finally something gave and he shot into the coach. I hoped he would not take the seat next to me, but he did.

He started to talk almost the moment he sat down, and he didn't stop until we reached Wallingford. Was I going to Choate? What a coincidence—so was he. My first year? His too. Where was I from? Oregon? No shit? Way the hell and gone up in the boondocks, eh? He was from Indiana—Gary, Indiana. I knew the song, didn't I? I did, but he sang it for me anyway, all the way through, including the tricky ending. There were other boys in the coach, and they were staring at us, and I wished he would shut up.

Did I swim? Too bad, it was a good sport, I ought to go out

for it. He had set a free-style record in the Midwestern conference the year before. What was my favorite subject? He liked math, he guessed, but he was pretty good at all of them. He offered me a cigarette, which I refused.

"I oughta quit myself," he said. "Be the death of me yet."

Eugene was a scholarship boy. One of his teachers told him that he was too smart to be going to a regular high school and gave him a list of prep schools. Eugene applied to all of them—"just for the hell of it"—and all of them accepted him. He finally decided on Choate because only Choate had offered him a travel allowance. His father was dead and his mother, a nurse, had three other kids to support, so Eugene didn't think it would be fair to ask her for anything. As the train came into Wallingford he asked me if I would be his roommate.

I didn't jump at the offer. For one thing, I did not like to look at Eugene. His head was too big for his lanky body, and his skin was oily. He put me in mind of a seal. Then there was the matter of his scholarship. I too was a scholarship boy, and I didn't want to finish myself off before I even got started by rooming with another, the way fat girls hung out together back home. I knew the world Eugene came from. I came from that world myself, and I wanted to leave it behind. To this end I had practiced over the summer an air of secret amusement which I considered to be aristocratic, an association encouraged by English movie actors. I had studied the photographs of the boys in the prep school bulletins, and now my hair looked like their hair and my clothes looked like their clothes.

I wanted to know boys whose fathers ran banks and held Cabinet offices and wrote books. I wanted to be their friend and go home with them on vacation and someday marry one of their sisters, and Eugene Miller didn't have much of a place in those plans. I told him that I had a friend at Choate with whom I'd probably be rooming.

"That's okay," he said. "Maybe next year."

I assented vaguely, and Eugene returned to the problem he was having deciding whether to go out for baseball or lacrosse. He was better at baseball, but lacrosse was more fun. He figured maybe he owed it to the school to go out for baseball.

As things worked out, our room assignments were already drawn up. My roommate was a Chilean named Jaime who described himself as a Nazi. He had an enormous poster of Adolf Hitler tacked above his desk until a Jewish boy on our hall complained and the dean made him take it down. Jaime kept a copy of *Mein Kampf* beside his bed like a Gideons Bible and was fond of reading aloud from it in a German accent. He enjoyed practical jokes. Our room overlooked the entrance to the headmaster's house and Jaime always whistled at the headmaster's ancient secretary as she went home from work at night. On Alumni Day he sneaked into the kitchen and spiced up the visitors' mock turtle soup with a number of condoms, unrolled and obscenely knotted. The next day at chapel the headmaster stammered out a sermon about the incident, but he referred to it in terms so coy and oblique that nobody knew what he was talking about. Ultimately the matter was dropped without another word. Just before Christmas Jaime's mother was killed in a plane crash, and he left school and never returned. For the rest of the year I roomed alone.

Eugene drew as his roommate Talbot Nevin. Talbot's family had donated the Andrew Nevin Memorial Hockey Rink and the Andrew Nevin Memorial Library to the school, and endowed the Andrew Nevin Memorial Lecture Series. Talbot Nevin's father had driven his car to second place in the Monaco Grand Prix two years earlier, and celebrity magazines often featured a picture of him with someone like Jill St. John and a caption underneath quoting one of them as saying, "We're just good friends." I wanted to know Talbot Nevin.

So one day I visited their room. Eugene met me at the door and pumped my hand. "Well, what do you know," he said. "Tab, this here's a buddy of mine from Oregon. You don't get any farther up in the boondocks than that."

Talbot Nevin sat on the edge of his bed, threading snow-white laces through the eyes of a pair of dirty sneakers. He nodded without raising his head.

"Tab's father won some big race last year," Eugene went on, to my discomfort. I didn't want Talbot to know that I had heard anything about him. I wanted to come to him fresh, with no possibility of his suspecting that I liked him for anything but himself.

"He didn't win. He came in second." Talbot threw down the sneakers and looked up at me for the first time. He had china-blue eyes under lashes and brows so light you could hardly see them. His hair too was shock-white and lank on his forehead. His face had a molded look, like a doll's face, delicate and unhealthy.

"What kind of race?" I asked.

"Grand Prix," he said, taking off his shoes.

"That's a car race," Eugene said.

Not to have heard of the Grand Prix seemed to me evidence of too great ignorance. "I know. I've heard of it."

"The guys down the hall were talking about it and they said he won." Eugene winked at me as he spoke; he winked continuously as if everything he said was part of a ritual joke and he didn't want a tenderfoot like me to take it too seriously.

"Well, I say he came in second and I damn well ought to know." By now Talbot had changed to his tennis shoes. He stood. "Let's go have a weed."

Smoking at Choate was forbidden. "The use of tobacco in any form," said the student handbook, "carries with it the penalty of immediate expulsion." Up to this moment the rule against smoking had not been a problem for me because I did not smoke. Now it was a problem, because I did not want Eugene to have a bond with Talbot that I did not share. So I followed them downstairs to the music room, where the choir practiced. Behind the conductor's platform was a long, narrow closet where the robes were kept. We huddled in the far end of this closet and Talbot passed out cigarettes. The risk was great and the activity silly, and we started to giggle.

"Welcome to Marlboro Country," I said.

"It's what's up front that counts," Talbot answered. We were smoking Marlboros, not Winstons, and the joke was lame, but I guffawed anyway.

"Better keep it down," Eugene whispered. "Big John might hear us."

Big John was the senior dorm master. He wore three-piece suits and soft-soled shoes and had a way of popping up at awkward moments. He liked to grab boys by the neck, pinching the skin between his forefinger and thumb, squeezing until they cried. "Fuck Big John," I said.

Neither Talbot nor Eugene responded. I fretted in the silence as we finished our cigarettes. I had intended to make Eugene look timid. Had I made myself look frivolous instead?

I saw Talbot several times that week and he barely nodded to me. I had been rash, I decided. I had made a bad impression on him. But on Friday night he came up as we were leaving the dining hall and asked me if I wanted to play tennis the next morning. I doubt that I have ever felt such complete self-satisfaction as I felt that night.

Talbot missed our appointment, however, so I dropped by

his room. He was still in bed, reading. "What's going on?" he asked, without looking up from his book.

I sat on Eugene's bed and tried not to sound as disappointed as I was. "I thought we might play a little tennis."

"Tennis?" He continued reading silently for a few moments. "I don't know. I don't feel so hot."

"No big deal. I thought you wanted to play. We could just knock a couple of balls around."

"Hell." He lowered the book onto his chest. "What time is it?"

"Nine o'clock."

"The courts'll be full by now."

"There's always a few empty ones behind the science building."

"They're asphalt, aren't they?"

"Cement." I shrugged. I didn't want to seem pushy. "Like I said, no big deal. We can play some other time." I stood and walked toward the door.

"Wait." Talbot yawned without covering his mouth. "What the hell."

As it happened, the courts were full. Talbot and I sat on the grass and I asked him questions I already knew the answers to, like where was he from and where had he gone to school the year before and who did he have for English. At this question he came to life. "English? Parker, the bald one. I got A's all through school and now Parker tells me I can't write. If he's such a goddamned William Shakespeare what's he teaching here for?"

We sat for a time without speaking. "I'm from Oregon," I said finally. "Near Portland." We didn't live close enough to the city to call it near, I suppose, but in those days I naively assumed everyone had heard of Portland.

"Oregon." He pondered this. "Do you hunt?"

"I've been a few times with my father."

"What kind of weapon do you use?"

"Marlin."

"30–30?"

I nodded.

"Good brush gun," he said. "Useless over a hundred yards. Have you ever killed anything?"

"Deer, you mean?"

"Deer, elk, whatever you hunt in Oregon."

"No."

Talbot had killed a lot of animals, and he named them for me: deer, moose, bear, elk, even an alligator. There were more, many more.

"Maybe you can come out West and go hunting with us sometime."

"Where, to Oregon?" Talbot looked away. "Maybe."

I had not expected to be humiliated on the court. My brother, who played tennis for Oregon State, had coached me through four summers. I had a good hot serve and my brother described my net game as "ruthless." Talbot ran me ragged. He played a kind of tennis different from any I had ever seen. He did not sweat, not the way I did anyway, or pant, or swear when he missed a shot, or get that thin quivering smile that tugged my lips whenever I aced my opponents. He seemed hardly to notice me, gave no sign that he was competing except that twice he called shots out that appeared to me to be well short of the line. I might have been mistaken, though. After he won the second set he walked abruptly off the court and went back to where we had left our sweaters. I followed him.

"Good game," I said.

He pulled impatiently at the sleeve of his sweater. "I can't play on these lousy asphalt courts."

Eugene made himself known around school. You did not wear belted jackets at Choate, or white buck shoes. Certainly you did not wear Alpine hats with feathers stuck in the brim. Eugene wore all three.

Anyone who didn't know who Eugene was found out by mid-November. *Life* magazine ran a series of interviews and pictures showing what it was like to be a student at a typical Eastern prep school. They had based their piece on research done at five schools, of which ours was one. Eugene had been interviewed and one of his remarks appeared in boldface beneath a photograph of students bent morosely over their books in evening study hall. The quotation: "One thing, nobody at Choate ever seems to smile. They think you're weird or something if you smile. You get dumped on all the time."

True enough. We were a joyless lot. Laughter was acceptable only in the sentimental parts of the movies we were shown on alternate Saturday nights. The one category in the yearbook to which everyone aspired was "Most Sarcastic." The arena for these trials of wit was the dining room, and Eugene's statements in *Life* did nothing to ease his load there.

However conspicuous Eugene may have been, he was not unpopular. I never heard anything worse about him than that he was "weird." He did well in his studies, and after the swimming team began to practice, the word went around that Eugene promised to put Choate in the running for the championship. So despite his hat and his eagerness and his determined grin, Eugene escaped the fate I had envisioned for him: the other students dumped on him but they didn't cast him out.

The night before school recessed for Christmas I went up to visit Talbot and found Eugene alone in the room, packing his bags. He made me sit down and poured out a glass of Hawaiian Punch which he laced with some murky substance from a prescription bottle. "Tab rustled up some codeine down at the infirmary," he explained. "This'll get the old Yule log burning."

The stuff tasted filthy but I took it, as I did all the other things that made the rounds at school and were supposed to get you off but never did, like aspirin and Coke, after-shave lotion, and Ben-Gay stuffed in the nostrils. "Where's Talbot?"

"I don't know. Maybe over at the library." He reached under his bed and pulled out a trunk-sized suitcase, made of cardboard but tricked up to look like leather, and began filling it with an assortment of pastel shirts with tab collars. Tab collars were another of Eugene's flings at sartorial trailblazing at school. They made me think of what my mother always told my sister when she complained at having to wear Mother's cast-off clothes: "You never know, you might start a fashion."

"Where are you going for Christmas?" Eugene asked.

"Baltimore."

"Baltimore? What's in Baltimore?"

"My aunt and uncle live there. How about you?"

"I'm heading on up to Boston."

This surprised me. I had assumed he would return to Indiana for the holidays. "Who do you know in Boston?"

"Nobody. Just Tab is all."

"Talbot? You're going to be staying with Talbot?"

"Yeah. And his family, of course."

"For the whole vacation?"

Eugene gave a sly grin and rolled his eyes from side to side and said in a confidential tone, almost a whisper: "Old Tab's got himself an extra key nobody knows about to his daddy's liquor closet. We aim to do some very big drinking. And I mean very big."

I went to the door. "If I don't see you in the morning, have a Merry Christmas."

"You bet, buddy. Same to you." Eugene grabbed my right hand in both of his. His fingers were soft and damp. "Take it easy on those Baltimore girls. Don't do anything I wouldn't do."

Jaime had been called home the week before by his mother's death. His bed was stripped, the mattress doubled over. All the pictures in the room had gone with him, and the yellow walls glared blankly. I turned out the lights and sat on my bed until the bell rang for dinner.

I had never met my aunt or uncle before. They picked me up at the station in Baltimore with their four children, three girls and a boy. I disliked all of them immediately. During the drive home my aunt asked me if my poor father had ever learned to cope with my mother's moods. One of the girls, Pammy, fell asleep on my lap and drooled on me.

They lived in Sherwood Park, a brick suburb several miles outside the city. My aunt and uncle went out almost every night and left me in charge of the children. This meant turning the television set on and turning it off when they had all passed out in front of it. Putting them to bed any earlier wasn't in the cards. They held on to everything—carpets, electrical cords, the legs of tables and chairs—and when that failed tried to injure themselves by scratching and gouging at their own faces.

One night I broke down. I cried for almost an hour and tried to call Talbot to ask him if I could come up to Boston and stay with him. The Nevins' number was unlisted, however, and after I washed my face and considered the idea again, I thought better of it.

When I returned to school my aunt and uncle wrote my father a letter which he sent on to me. They said that I was selfish and unenterprising. They had welcomed me as a son. They had opened their hearts to me, but I had taken no interest in them or in their children, my cousins, who worshipped the very ground I walked on. They cited an incident when I was in the kitchen reading and the wind blew all my aunt's laundry off the line and I hadn't so much as *asked* if I could help. I just sat there and went right on reading and eating peanuts. Finally, my uncle was missing a set of cuff links that had great sentimental value for him. All things considered, they didn't think my coming to Baltimore had worked out very well. They thought that on future vacations I would be happier somewhere else.

I wrote back to my father, denying all charges and making a few of my own.

After Christmas Talbot and I were often together. Both of us had gone out for basketball, and as neither of us was any good to the team—Talbot because of an ankle injury, I because I couldn't make the ball go through the basket—we sat together on the bench most of the time. He told me Eugene had spoiled his stepmother's Christmas by leaning back in an antique chair and breaking it. Thereafter I thought of Mrs. Nevin as a friend; but I had barely a month to enjoy the alliance because in late January Talbot told me that his father and stepmother had separated.

Eugene was taken up with swimming, and I saw him rarely. Talbot and I had most of our friends among the malcontents in the school: those, like Talbot, to whom every rule gave offense; those who missed their girl friends or their cars; and those, like me, who knew that something was wrong but didn't know what it was.

Because I was not rich my dissatisfaction could not assume a really combative form. I paddled around on the surface, dabbling in revolt by way of the stories I wrote for *off the record*, the school literary journal. My stories took place at "The Hoatch School" and concerned a student from the West whom I referred to simply as "the boy."

The boy's father came from a distinguished New York family. In his early twenties, he had traveled to Oregon to oversee his family's vast lumber holdings. His family turned on him when he married a beautiful young woman who happened to be part Indian. The Indian blood was noble, but the boy's father was disowned anyway.

The boy's parents prospered in spite of this and raised a large, gifted family. The boy was the most gifted of all, and his father sent him back East to Hoatch, the traditional family school. What he found there saddened him: among the students a preoccupation with money and social position, and among the masters hypocrisy and pettiness. The boy's only friends were a beautiful young dancer who worked as a waitress in a café near the school, and an old tramp. The dancer and tramp were referred to as "the girl" and "the tramp." The boy and girl were forever getting the tramp out of trouble for doing things like painting garbage cans beautiful colors.

I doubt that Talbot ever read my stories—he never mentioned them if he did—but somehow he got the idea I was a writer. One night he came to my room and dropped a notebook on my desk and asked me to read the essay inside. It was on the topic "Why Is Literature Worth Studying?" and it sprawled over four pages, concluding as follows:

I think Literature is worth studying but only in a way. The people of our Country should know how intelligent the people of past history were. They should appreciate what gifts these people had to write such great works of

Literature. This is why I think Literature is worth studying.

Talbot had received an F on the essay.

"Parker says he's going to put me in summer school if I flunk
again this marking period," Talbot said, lighting a cigarette.

"I didn't know you flunked last time." I stared helplessly at
the cigarette. "Maybe you shouldn't smoke. Big John might
smell it."

"I saw Big John going into the library on my way over here."
Talbot went to the mirror and examined his profile from the
corner of his eye. "I thought maybe you could help me out."

"How?"

"Maybe give me a few ideas. You ought to see the topics he
gives us. Like this one." He took some folded papers from his
back pocket. "'Describe the most interesting person you
know.'" He swore and threw the papers down.

I picked them up. "What's this? Your outline?"

"More like a rough draft, I guess you'd call it."

I read the essay. The writing was awful, but what really
shocked me was the absolute lack of interest with which he
described the most interesting person he had ever known. This
person turned out to be his English teacher from the year before, whose chief virtue seemed to be that he gave a lot of
reading periods and didn't expect his students to be William
Shakespeare and write him a novel every week.

"I don't think Parker is going to like this very much," I said.

"Why? What's wrong with it?"

"He might get the idea you're trying to criticize him."

"That's his problem."

I folded up the essay and handed it back to Talbot with his
notebook.

"You really think he'll give me an F on it?"

"He might."

Talbot crumpled the essay. "Hell."

"When is it due?"

"Tomorrow."

"Tomorrow?"

"I'd have come over before this but I've been busy."

We spent the next hour or so talking about other interesting people he had known. There weren't many of them, and the only one who really interested me was a maid named Tina who used to masturbate Talbot when she tucked him in at night and was later arrested for trying to burn the Nevins' house down. Talbot couldn't remember anything about her though, not even her last name. We finally abandoned what promise Tina held of suggesting an essay.

What eventually happened was that I got up at four-thirty next morning and invented a fictional interesting person for Talbot. This person's name was Miles and he was supposed to have been one of Talbot's uncles.

I gave the essay to Talbot outside the dining hall. He read it without expression. "I don't have any Uncle Miles," he said. "I don't have any uncles at all. Just aunts."

"Parker doesn't know that."

"But it was supposed to be about someone interesting." He was frowning at the essay. "I don't see what's so interesting about this guy."

"If you don't want to use it I will."

"That's okay. I'll use it."

I wrote three more essays for Talbot in the following weeks: "Who Is Worse—Macbeth or Lady Macbeth?"; "Is There a God?"; and "Describe a Fountain Pen to a Person Who Has Never Seen One." Mr. Parker read the last essay aloud to Talbot's class as an example of clear expository writing and put a note on the back of the essay saying how pleased he was to see Talbot getting down to work.

In late February the dean put a notice on the bulletin board: those students who wished to room together the following year had to submit their names to him by Friday. There was no time to waste. I went immediately to Talbot's dorm.

Eugene was alone in the room, stuffing dirty clothes into a canvas bag. He came toward me, winking and grinning and snorting. "Hey there, buddy, how they hangin'? Side-by-side for comfort or back-to-back for speed?"

We had sat across from each other at breakfast, lunch, and dinner every day now for three weeks, and each time we met he behaved as if we were brothers torn by Arabs from each other's arms and just now reunited after twenty years.

"Where's Talbot?" I asked.

"He had a phone call. Be back pretty soon."

"Aren't you supposed to be at swimming practice?"

"Not today." He smirked mysteriously.

"Why not?"

"I broke the conference butterfly record yesterday. Against Kent."

"That's great. Congratulations."

"And butterfly isn't even my best stroke. Hey, good thing you came over. I was just about to go see you."

"What about?"

"I was wondering who you were planning on rooming with next year."

"Oh, well, you know, I sort of promised this other guy."

Eugene nodded, still smiling. "Fair enough. I already had someone ask me. I just thought I'd check with you first. Since we didn't have a chance to room together this year." He stood and resumed stuffing the pile of clothes in his bag. "Is it three o'clock yet?"

"Quarter to."

"I guess I better get these duds over to the cleaners before they close. See you later, buddy."

Talbot came back to the room a few minutes afterward. "Where's Eugene?"

"He was taking some clothes to the cleaners."

"Oh." Talbot drew a cigarette from the pack he kept hidden under the washstand and lit it. "Here," he said, passing it to me.

"Just a drag." I puffed at it and handed it back. I decided to come to the point. "Who are you rooming with next year?"

"Eugene."

"*Eugene?*"

"He has to check with somebody else first but he thinks it'll be all right." Talbot picked up his squash racket and hefted it. "How about you?"

"I don't know. I kind of like rooming alone."

"More privacy," said Talbot, swinging the racket in a broad backhand.

"That's right. More privacy."

"Maybe that South American guy will come back."

"I doubt it."

"You never know. His old man might get better."

"It's his mother. And she's dead."

"Oh." Talbot kept swinging the racket, forehand now.

"By the way, there's something I meant to tell you."

"What's that?"

"I'm not going to be able to help you with those essays anymore."

He shrugged. "Okay."

"I've got enough work of my own to do. I can't do my work and yours too."

"I said okay. Parker can't flunk me now anyway. I've got a C+ average."

"I just thought I'd tell you."

"So you told me." Talbot finished the cigarette and stashed the butt in a tin soap dish. "We'd better go. We're gonna be late for basketball."

"I'm not going to basketball."

"Why not?"

"Because I don't feel like going to basketball, that's why not."

We left the building together and split up at the bottom of the steps without exchanging another word. I went down to the infirmary to get an excuse for not going to basketball. The doctor was out and I had to wait for an hour until he came back and gave me some pills and Kaopectate. When I got back to my room the dorm was in an uproar.

I heard the story from the boys in the room next to mine. Big John had caught Eugene smoking. He had come into Eugene's room and found him there alone and smelled cigarette smoke. Eugene had denied it but Big John tore the room apart and found cigarettes and butts all over the place. Eugene was over at the headmaster's house at this moment.

They told me the story in a mournful way, as though they were really broken up about it, but I could see how excited they were. It was always like that when someone got kicked out of school.

I went to my room and pulled a chair over to the window. Just before the bell rang for dinner a taxi came up the drive. Big John walked out of the dorm with two enormous cardboard suitcases and helped the driver put them in the trunk.

He gave the driver some money and said something to him and the driver nodded and got back into the cab. Then the head-master and the dean came out of the house with Eugene be-hind them. Eugene was wearing his hat. He shook hands with both of them and then with Big John. Suddenly he bent over and put his hands up to his face. The dean reached out and touched his arm. They stood like that for a long time, the four of them, Eugene's shoulders bucking and heaving. I couldn't watch it. I went to the mirror and combed my hair until I heard the door of the taxi bang shut. When I looked out the window again the cab was gone. The headmaster and the dean were standing in the shadows, but I could see Big John clearly. He was rocking back on his heels and talking, hands on his hips, and something he said made the headmaster laugh; not really a laugh, more like a giggle. The only thing I heard was the word "feathers." I figured they must be talking about Eu-gene's hat. Then the bell rang and the three of them went into the dining hall.

The next day I walked by the dean's office and almost went in and told him everything. The problem was, if I told the dean about Talbot he would find out about me, too. The rules didn't set forth different punishments according to the amount of smoke consumed. I even considered sending the dean an anonymous note, but I doubted if it would get much attention. They were big on doing the gentlemanly thing at Choate.

On Friday Talbot came up to me at basketball practice and asked if I wanted to room with him next year.

"I'll think about it," I told him.

"The names have to be in by dinner time tonight."

"I said I'll think about it."

That evening Talbot submitted our names to the dean. There hadn't really been that much to think about. For all I know, Eugene *had* been smoking when Big John came into the room. If you wanted to get technical about it, he was guilty as charged a hundred times over. It wasn't as if some great injustice had been done.

Wingfield

When we arrived at the camp they pulled us off the buses and made us do push-ups in the parking lot. The asphalt was hot and tar stuck to our noses. They made fun of our clothes and took them away from us. They shaved our heads until little white scars showed through, then filled our arms with boots and belts and helmets and punctured them with needles.

In the middle of the night they came to our barracks and walked up and down between us as we stood by our bunks. They looked at us. If we looked at them they said, "Why are you looking at me?" and made us do push-ups. If you didn't act right they made your life sad.

They divided us into companies, platoons, and squads. In my squad were Wingfield and Parker and seven others. Parker was a wise guy, my friend. I never saw anything get him down except malaria. Wingfield, before the military took responsibility for him, had been kept alive somewhere in North Carolina. When he was in a condition to talk his voice oozed out of him thick and slow and sweet. His eyes when he had them open were the palest blue. Most of the time they were closed.

He often fell asleep while he polished his boots, and once while he was shaving. They ordered him to paint baseboards and he curled up in the corner and let the baseboards take care of themselves. They found him with his head resting on his outstretched arm, his mouth open; a string of paint had dried between the brush and the floor.

In the afternoons they showed us films: from these we learned how to maintain our jeeps, how to protect our teeth from decay, how to treat foreigners, and how to sheathe ourselves against boils, nervous disorders, madness, and finally the long night of the blind. The foreigners wore shiny suits and carried briefcases. They smiled as they directed our soldiers to their destinations. They would do the same for us if we could remember how to ask them questions. As we repeated the important phrases to ourselves we could hear the air whistling in and out of Wingfield's mouth, rattling in the depths of his throat.

Wingfield slept as they showed us how our weapons worked, and what plants we could browse on if we got lost or ran out of food. Sometimes they caught him and made him stand up; he would smile shyly, like a young girl, and find something to lean against, and go back to sleep. He slept while we marched, which other soldiers could do; but other soldiers marched straight when they were supposed to turn and turned when they were supposed to march straight. They marched into trees and ditches and walls, they fell into holes. Wingfield could march around corners while asleep. He could sing the cadence and double-time at port arms without opening his eyes. You had to see it to believe it.

At the end of our training they drove us deep into the woods and set our company against another. To make the numbers even they gave the other side six of our men, Wingfield among them. He did not want to go but they made him. Then they handed out blank ammunition and colored scarves, blue for us and red for them.

The presence of these two colors made the woods dangerous. We tiptoed from bush to bush, crawled on our stomachs through brown needles under the stunted pines. The bark of the trees was sweating amber resin but you couldn't stop and stare. If you dawdled and daydreamed you would be taken in ambush. When soldiers with red scarves walked by we hid and shot them from behind and sent them to the parking lot, which was no longer a parking lot but the land of the dead.

A wind sprang up, bending and shaking the trees; their shadows lunged at us. Then darkness fell over the woods, sudden as a trap closing. Here and there we saw a stab of flame and heard a shot, but soon this scattered firing fell away. We pitched tents and posted guards; sat in silence and ate food from cans, cold. Our heartbeats echoed in our helmets.

Parker threw rocks. We heard them thumping the earth, breaking brittle branches as they fell. Someone yelled at him to stop, and Parker pointed where the shout came from.

Then we blackened our faces and taped our jingling dog tags, readied ourselves to raid. We slipped into the darkness as though we belonged there, like shadows. Gnats swarmed, mosquitos stung us but we did not slap; we were that stealthy. We went on until we saw, not far ahead, a fire. A fire! The fools had made a fire! Parker put his hand over his mouth and shook his head from side to side, signifying laughter. The rest of us did the same.

We only had to find the guards to take the camp by surprise. I found one right away, mumbling and exclaiming in his sleep, his rifle propped against a tree. It was Wingfield. With hatred and contempt and joy I took him from behind, and as I drew it across his throat I was wishing that my finger was a knife.

Twisting in my arms, he looked into my black face and said, "Oh my God," as though I was no impostor but Death himself.

Then we stormed the camp, firing into the figures lumped in sleeping bags, firing into the tents and into the shocked white faces at the tent flaps. It was exactly the same thing that happened to us a year and three months later as we slept beside a canal in the Mekong Delta, a few kilometers from Ben Tré.

We were sent home on leave when our training ended, and when we regrouped, several of us were missing, sick or AWOL or sent overseas to fill the ranks of units picked clean in the latest fighting. Wingfield was among them. I never saw him again and I never expected to. From now on his nights would be filled with shadows like me, and against such enemies what chance did Wingfield have?

Parker got malaria two weeks before the canal attack, and was still in the hospital when it happened. When he got out they sent him to another unit. He wrote letters to me but I never answered them. They were full of messages for people who weren't alive anymore, and I thought it would be a good thing if he never knew this. Then he would lose only one friend instead of twenty-six. At last the letters stopped and I did not hear from him again for nine years, when he knocked on my door one evening just after I'd come home from work.

He had written my parents, he explained, and they had told him where I was living. He said that he and his wife and daughter were just passing through on their way to Canada, but I knew better. There were other ways to go than this and travelers always took them. He wanted an accounting.

Parker's daughter played with my dogs and his wife cooked steaks in the barbecue pit while we drank beer and talked and looked each other over. He was still cheerful, but in a softer, slower way, like a jovial uncle of the boy he'd been. After we ate we lay on the blanket until the bugs got to our ankles and the child began to whine. Parker's wife carried the dishes into the house and washed them while we settled on the steps. The light from the kitchen window laid a garish patch upon the lawn. Things crawled toward it under the grass. Parker asked the question he'd come to ask and then sat back and waited while I spoke name after name into the night. When I finished he said, "Is that all? What about Washington?"

"I told you. He got home all right."

"You're sure about that?"

"Of course I'm sure."

"You ought to get married," Parker said, standing up. "You take yourself too seriously. What the hell, right?"

Parker's daughter was lying on the living-room floor next to my golden retriever, who growled softly in his sleep as Parker lifted the girl and slung her over his shoulder. His wife took my arm and leaned against me as we walked out to the car. "I feel so comfortable with you," she said. "You remind me of my grandfather."

"By the way," Parker said, "do you remember Wingfield?"

"He was with that first bunch that got sent over," I said. "I don't think he made it back."

"Who told you that?"

"Nobody. I just don't think he did."

"You're wrong. I saw him." Parker shifted the girl to his other shoulder. "That's what I was going to tell you. I was in Charlotte six months ago and I saw him in the train station, sitting on a bench."

"You didn't."

"Oh, yes, I did."

"How was he? What did he say?"

"He didn't say anything. I was in a hurry and he looked so peaceful I just couldn't bring myself to wake him up."

"But it was definitely him?"

"It was Wingfield all right. He had his mouth open."

I waved at their car until it made the turn at the end of the street. Then I rummaged through the garbage and filled the dogs' bowls with the bones and gristle Parker's wife had thrown away. As I inspected the dishes she had washed the thought came to me that this was a fussy kind of thing for a young man to do.

I opened a bottle of wine and went outside. The coals in the cooking pit hissed and flushed as the wind played over them, pulling away the smoke in tight spirals. I sensed the wings of the bats above me, wheeling in the darkness. Like a soldier on leave, like a boy who knows nothing at all, like a careless and go-to-hell fellow I drank to them. Then I drank to the crickets and locusts and cicadas who purred so loudly that the earth itself seemed to be snoring. I drank to the snoring earth, to the closed eye of the moon, to the trees that nodded and sighed: until, already dreaming, I fell back upon the blanket.

In the Garden of the
North American
Martyrs

When she was young, Mary saw a brilliant and original man lose his job because he had expressed ideas that were offensive to the trustees of the college where they both taught. She shared his views, but did not sign the protest petition. She was, after all, on trial herself—as a teacher, as a woman, as an interpreter of history.

Mary watched herself. Before giving a lecture she wrote it out in full, using the arguments and often the words of other, approved writers, so that she would not by chance say something scandalous. Her own thoughts she kept to herself, and the words for them grew faint as time went on; without quite disappearing they shrank to remote, nervous points, like birds flying away.

When the department turned into a hive of cliques, Mary went about her business and pretended not to know that people hated each other. To avoid seeming bland she let herself become eccentric in harmless ways. She took up bowling, which she learned to love, and founded the Brandon College chapter of a society dedicated to restoring the good name of Richard III. She memorized comedy routines from records and jokes from books; people groaned when she rattled them off, but she did not let that stop her, and after a time the groans became the point of the jokes. They were a kind of tribute to Mary's willingness to expose herself.

In fact no one at the college was safer than Mary, for she was making herself into something institutional, like a custom, or a mascot—part of the college's idea of itself.

Now and then she wondered whether she had been too careful. The things she said and wrote seemed flat to her, pulpy, as though someone else had squeezed the juice out of them. And once, while talking with a senior professor, Mary saw herself reflected in a window: she was leaning toward him and had her head turned so that her ear was right in front of his moving mouth. The sight disgusted her. Years later, when she had to get a hearing aid, Mary suspected that her deafness was a result of always trying to catch everything everyone said.

In the second half of Mary's fifteenth year at Brandon the provost called a meeting of all faculty and students to announce that the college was bankrupt and would not open its gates again. He was every bit as much surprised as they; the report from the trustees had reached his desk only that morning. It seemed that Brandon's financial manager had speculated in some kind of futures and lost everything. The provost wanted to deliver the news in person before it reached the papers. He wept openly and so did the students and teachers, with only a few exceptions—some cynical upperclassmen who claimed to despise the education they had received.

Mary could not rid her mind of the word "speculate." It meant to guess, in terms of money to gamble. How could a man gamble a college? Why would he want to do that, and how could it be that no one stopped him? To Mary, it seemed to belong to another time; she thought of a drunken plantation owner gaming away his slaves.

She applied for jobs and got an offer from a new experimental college in Oregon. It was her only offer so she took it.

The college was in one building. Bells rang all the time, lockers lined the hallways, and at every corner stood a buzzing water fountain. The student newspaper came out twice a month on mimeograph paper which felt wet. The library, which was next to the band room, had no librarian and no books.

The countryside was beautiful, though, and Mary might have enjoyed it if the rain had not caused her so much trouble. There was something wrong with her lungs that the doctors couldn't agree on, and couldn't cure; whatever it was, the dampness made it worse. On rainy days condensation formed in Mary's hearing aid and shorted it out. She began to dread talking with people, never knowing when she would have to take out her control box and slap it against her leg.

It rained nearly every day. When it was not raining it was getting ready to rain, or clearing. The ground glinted under the grass, and the light had a yellow undertone that flared up during storms.

There was water in Mary's basement. Her walls sweated, and she had found toadstools growing behind the refrigerator. She felt as though she were rusting out, like one of those old cars people thereabouts kept in their front yards, on pieces of wood. Mary knew that everyone was dying, but it did seem to her that she was dying faster than most.

She continued to look for another job, without success. Then, in the fall of her third year in Oregon, she got a letter from a woman named Louise who'd once taught at Brandon. Louise had scored a great success with a book on Benedict Arnold and was now on the faculty of a famous college in upstate New York. She said that one of her colleagues would be retiring at the end of the year and asked whether Mary would be interested in the position.

The letter surprised Mary. Louise thought of herself as a great historian and of almost everyone else as useless; Mary had not known that she felt differently about her. Moreover, enthusiasm for other people's causes did not come easily to Louise, who had a way of sucking in her breath when familiar names were mentioned, as though she knew things that friendship kept her from disclosing.

Mary expected nothing, but sent a résumé and copies of her two books. Shortly after that Louise called to say that the search committee, of which she was chairwoman, had decided to grant Mary an interview in early November. "Now don't get your hopes *too* high," Louise said.

"Oh, no," Mary said, but thought: Why shouldn't I hope? They would not go to the bother and expense of bringing her to the college if they weren't serious. And she was certain that the interview would go well. She would make them like her, or at least give them no cause to dislike her.

She read about the area with a strange sense of familiarity, as if the land and its history were already known to her. And when her plane left Portland and climbed easterly into the clouds, Mary felt like she was going home. The feeling stayed with her, growing stronger when they landed. She tried to describe it to Louise as they left the airport at Syracuse and drove toward the college, an hour or so away. "It's like *déjà vu*," she said.

"*Déjà vu* is a hoax," Louise said. "It's just a chemical imbalance of some kind."

"Maybe so," Mary said, "but I still have this sensation."

"Don't get serious on me," Louise said. "That's not your long suit. Just be your funny, wisecracking old self. Tell me now—honestly—how do I look?"

It was night, too dark to see Louise's face well, but in the airport she had seemed gaunt and pale and intense. She reminded Mary of a description in the book she'd been reading, of how Iroquois warriors gave themselves visions by fasting. She had that kind of look about her. But she wouldn't want to hear that. "You look wonderful," Mary said.

"There's a reason," Louise said. "I've taken a lover. My concentration has improved, my energy level is up, and I've lost ten pounds. I'm also getting some color in my cheeks, though that could be the weather. I recommend the experience highly. But you probably disapprove."

Mary didn't know what to say. She said that she was sure Louise knew best, but that didn't seem to be enough. "Marriage is a great institution," she added, "but who wants to live in an institution?"

Louise groaned. "I know you," she said, "and I know that right now you're thinking 'But what about Ted? What about the children?' The fact is, Mary, they aren't taking it well at all. Ted has become a nag." She handed Mary her purse. "Be a good girl and light me a cigarette, will you? I know I told you I quit, but this whole thing has been very hard on me, very hard, and I'm afraid I've started again."

They were in the hills now, heading north on a narrow road. Tall trees arched above them. As they topped a rise Mary saw the forest all around, deep black under the plum-colored sky. There were a few lights and these made the darkness seem even greater.

"Ted has succeeded in completely alienating the children from me," Louise was saying. "There is no reasoning with any of them. In fact, they refuse to discuss the matter at all, which is very ironical because over the years I have tried to instill in them a willingness to see things from the other person's point of view. If they could just *meet* Jonathan I know they would feel differently. But they won't hear of it. Jonathan," she said, "is my lover."

"I see," Mary said, and nodded.

Coming around a curve they caught two deer in the headlights. Their eyes lit up and their hindquarters tensed; Mary could see them trembling as the car went by. "Deer," she said.

"I don't know," Louise said, "I just don't know. I do my best and it never seems to be enough. But that's enough about me—let's talk about you. What did you think of my latest book?" She squawked and beat her palms on the steering wheel. "God, I love that joke," she said. "Seriously, though, what about you? It must have been a real shockeroo when good old Brandon folded."

"It was hard. Things haven't been good but they'll be a lot better if I get this job."

"At least you have work," Louise said. "You should look at it from the bright side."

"I try."

"You seem so gloomy. I hope you're not worrying about the interview, or the class. Worrying won't do you a bit of good. Be happy."

"Class? What class?"

"The class you're supposed to give tomorrow, after the interview. Didn't I tell you? *Mea culpa*, hon, *mea maxima culpa*. I've been uncharacteristically forgetful lately."

"But what will I do?"

"Relax," Louise said. "Just pick a subject and wing it."

"Wing it?"

"You know, open your mouth and see what comes out. Extemporize."

"But I always work from a prepared lecture."

Louise sighed. "All right. I'll tell you what. Last year I wrote an article on the Marshall Plan that I got bored with and never published. You can read that."

Parroting what Louise had written seemed wrong to Mary, at first; then it occurred to her that she had been doing the same kind of thing for many years, and that this was not the time to get scruples. "Thanks," she said. "I appreciate it."

"Here we are," Louise said, and pulled into a circular drive with several cabins grouped around it. In two of the cabins lights were on; smoke drifted straight up from the chimneys. "This is the visitors' center. The college is another two miles thataway." Louise pointed down the road. "I'd invite you to stay at my house, but I'm spending the night with Jonathan and Ted is not good company these days. You would hardly recognize him."

She took Mary's bags from the trunk and carried them up the steps of a darkened cabin. "Look," she said, "they've laid a fire for you. All you have to do is light it." She stood in the middle of the room with her arms crossed and watched as Mary held a match under the kindling. "There," she said. "You'll be snugaroo in no time. I'd love to stay and chew the fat but I can't. You just get a good night's sleep and I'll see you in the morning."

Mary stood in the doorway and waved as Louise pulled out of the drive, spraying gravel. She filled her lungs, to taste the air: it was tart and clear. She could see the stars in their figurations, and the vague streams of light that ran among the stars.

She still felt uneasy about reading Louise's work as her own. It would be her first complete act of plagiarism. It would change her. It would make her less—how much less, she did not know. But what else could she do? She certainly couldn't "wing it." Words might fail her, and then what? Mary had a dread of silence. When she thought of silence she thought of drowning, as if it were a kind of water she could not swim in.

"I want this job," she said, and settled deep into her coat. It was cashmere and Mary had not worn it since moving to Oregon, because people there thought you were pretentious if you had on anything but a Pendleton shirt or, of course, rain-gear. She rubbed her cheek against the upturned collar and thought of a silver moon shining through bare black branches, a white house with green shutters, red leaves falling in a hard blue sky.

L ouise woke her a few hours later. She was sitting on the ledge of the bed, pushing at Mary's shoulder and snuffling loudly. When Mary asked her what was wrong she said, "I want your opinion on something. It's very important. Do you think I'm womanly?"

Mary sat up. "Louise, can this wait?"

"No."

"Womanly?"

Louise nodded.

"You are very beautiful," Mary said, "and you know how to present yourself."

Louise stood and paced the room. "That son of a bitch," she said. She came back and stood over Mary. "Let's suppose someone said I have no sense of humor. Would you agree or disagree?"

"In some things you do. I mean, yes, you have a good sense of humor."

"What do you mean, 'in some things'? What kind of things?"

"Well, if you heard that someone had been killed in an un-usual way, like by an exploding cigar, you would think that was funny."

Louise laughed.

"That's what I mean," Mary said.

Louise went on laughing. "Oh, Lordy," she said. "Now it's my turn to say something about you." She sat down beside Mary.

"Please," Mary said.

"Just one thing," Louise said.

Mary waited.

"You're trembling," Louise said. "I was just going to say— oh, forget it. Listen, do you mind if I sleep on the couch? I'm all in."

"Go ahead."

"Sure it's okay? You've got a big day tomorrow." She fell back on the sofa and kicked off her shoes. "I was just going to say, you should use some liner on those eyebrows of yours. They sort of disappear and the effect is disconcerting."

Neither of them slept. Louise chain-smoked cigarettes and Mary watched the coals burn down. When it was light enough that they could see each other Louise got up. "I'll send a student for you," she said. "Good luck."

The college looked the way colleges are supposed to look. Roger, the student assigned to show Mary around, explained that it was an exact copy of a college in England, right down to the gargoyles and stained-glass windows. It looked so much like a college that moviemakers sometimes used it as a set. *Andy Hardy Goes to College* had been filmed there, and every fall they had an Andy Hardy Goes to College Day, with raccoon coats and goldfish-swallowing contests.

Above the door of the Founder's Building was a Latin motto which, roughly translated, meant "God helps those who help themselves." As Roger recited the names of illustrious graduates Mary was struck by the extent to which they had taken this precept to heart. They had helped themselves to railroads, mines, armies, states; to empires of finance with outposts all over the world.

Roger took Mary to the chapel and showed her a plaque bearing the names of alumni who had been killed in various wars, all the way back to the Civil War. There were not many names. Here too, apparently, the graduates had helped themselves. "Oh, yes," Roger said as they were leaving, "I forgot to tell you. The communion rail comes from some church in Europe where Charlemagne used to go."

They went to the gymnasium, and the three hockey rinks, and the library, where Mary inspected the card catalogue, as though she would turn down the job if they didn't have the right books. "We have a little more time," Roger said as they went outside. "Would you like to see the power plant?"

Mary wanted to keep busy until the last minute, so she agreed.

Roger led her into the depths of the service building, explaining things about the machine, which was the most advanced in the country. "People think the college is really old-fashioned," he said, "but it isn't. They let girls come here now, and some of the teachers are women. In fact, there's a statute that says they have to interview at least one woman for each opening. There it is."

They were standing on an iron catwalk above the biggest machine Mary had ever beheld. Roger, who was majoring in Earth Sciences, said that it had been built from a design pioneered by a professor in his department. Where before he had been gabby Roger now became reverent. It was clear that for him this machine was the soul of the college, that the purpose of the college was to provide outlets for the machine. Together they leaned against the railing and watched it hum.

Mary arrived at the committee room exactly on time for her interview, but the room was empty. Her two books were on the table, along with a water pitcher and some glasses. She sat down and picked up one of the books. The binding cracked as she opened it. The pages were smooth, clean, unread. Mary turned to the first chapter, which began, "It is generally believed that . . ." How dull, she thought.

Nearly twenty minutes later Louise came in with several men. "Sorry we're late," she said. "We don't have much time so we'd better get started." She introduced Mary to the men, but with one exception the names and faces did not stay together. The exception was Dr. Howells, the department chairman, who had a porous blue nose and terrible teeth.

A shiny-faced man to Dr. Howells's right spoke first. "So," he said, "I understand you once taught at Brandon College."

"It was a shame that Brandon had to close," said a young man with a pipe in his mouth. "There is a place for schools like Brandon." As he talked the pipe wagged up and down.

"Now you're in Oregon," Dr. Howells said. "I've never been there. How do you like it?"

"Not very much," Mary said.

"Is that right?" Dr. Howells leaned toward her. "I thought everyone liked Oregon. I hear it's very green."

"That's true," Mary said.

"I suppose it rains a lot," he said.

"Nearly every day."

"I wouldn't like that," he said, shaking his head. "I like it dry. Of course it snows here, and you have your rain now and then, but it's a *dry* rain. Have you ever been to Utah? There's a state for you. Bryce Canyon. The Mormon Tabernacle Choir."

"Dr. Howells was brought up in Utah," said the young man with the pipe.

"It was a different place altogether in those days," Dr. Howells said. "Mrs. Howells and I have always talked about going back when I retire, but now I'm not so sure."

"We're a little short on time," Louise said.

"And here I've been going on and on," Dr. Howells said. "Before we wind things up, is there anything you want to tell us?"

"Yes. I think you should give me the job." Mary laughed when she said this, but no one laughed back, or even looked at her. They all looked away. Mary understood then that they were not really considering her for the position. She had been brought here to satisfy a rule. She had no hope.

The men gathered their papers and shook hands with Mary and told her how much they were looking forward to her class. "I can't get enough of the Marshall Plan," Dr. Howells said.

"Sorry about that," Louise said when they were alone. "I didn't think it would be so bad. That was a real bitcheroo."

"Tell me something," Mary said. "You already know who you're going to hire, don't you?"

Louise nodded.

"Then why did you bring me here?"

Louise began to explain about the statute and Mary interrupted. "I know all that. But why me? Why did you pick *me*?"

Louise walked to the window. She spoke with her back to Mary. "Things haven't been going very well for old Louise," she said. "I've been unhappy and I thought you might cheer me up. You used to be so funny, and I was sure you would enjoy the trip—it didn't cost you anything, and it's pretty this time of year with the leaves and everything. Mary, you don't know the things my parents did to me. And Ted is no barrel of laughs either. Or Jonathan, the son of a bitch. I deserve some love and friendship but I don't get any." She turned and looked at her watch. "It's almost time for your class. We'd better go."

"I would rather not give it. After all, there's not much point, is there?"

"But you *have* to give it. That's part of the interview." Louise handed Mary a folder. "All you have to do is read this. It isn't much, considering all the money we've laid out to get you here."

Mary followed Louise down the hall to the lecture room. The professors were sitting in the front row with their legs crossed. They smiled and nodded at Mary. Behind them the room was full of students, some of whom had spilled over into the aisles. One of the professors adjusted the microphone to Mary's height, crouching down as he went to the podium and back as though he would prefer not to be seen.

Louise called the room to order. She introduced Mary and gave the subject of the lecture. But Mary had decided to wing it after all. Mary came to the podium unsure of what she would say; sure only that she would rather die than read Louise's article. The sun poured through the stained glass onto the people around her, painting their faces. Thick streams of smoke from the young professor's pipe drifted through a circle of red light at Mary's feet, turning crimson and twisting like flames.

"I wonder how many of you know," she began, "that we are in the Long House, the ancient domain of the Five Nations of the Iroquois."

Two professors looked at each other.

"The Iroquois were without pity," Mary said. "They hunted people down with clubs and arrows and spears and nets, and blowguns made from elder stalks. They tortured their captives, sparing no one, not even the little children. They took scalps and practiced cannibalism and slavery. Because they had no pity they became powerful, so powerful that no other tribe dared to oppose them. They made the other tribes pay tribute, and when they had nothing more to pay the Iroquois attacked them."

Several of the professors began to whisper. Dr. Howells was saying something to Louise, and Louise was shaking her head.

"In one of their raids," Mary said, "they captured two Jesuit priests, Jean de Brébeuf and Gabriel Lalement. They covered Lalement with pitch and set him on fire in front of Brébeuf. When Brébeuf rebuked them they cut off his lips and put a burning iron down his throat. They hung a collar of red-hot hatchets around his neck, and poured boiling water over his head. When he continued to preach to them they cut strips of flesh from his body and ate them before his eyes. While he was still alive they scalped him and cut open his breast and drank his blood. Later, their chief tore out Brébeuf's heart and ate it, but just before he did this Brébeuf spoke to them one last time. He said—"

"That's enough!" yelled Dr. Howells, jumping to his feet.

Louise stopped shaking her head. Her eyes were perfectly round.

Mary had come to the end of her facts. She did not know what Brébeuf had said. Silence rose up around her; just when she thought she would go under and be lost in it she heard someone whistling in the hallway outside, trilling the notes like a bird, like many birds.

"Mend your lives," she said. "You have deceived yourselves in the pride of your hearts, and the strength of your arms. Though you soar aloft like the eagle, though your nest is set among the stars, thence I will bring you down, says the Lord. Turn from power to love. Be kind. Do justice. Walk humbly."

Louise was waving her arms. "Mary!" she shouted.

But Mary had more to say, much more; she waved back at Louise, then turned off her hearing aid so that she would not be distracted again.

Poaching

W harton was a cartoonist, and a nervous man—"high-strung," he would have said. Because of his occupation and his nerves he required peace, but in Vancouver he didn't get much of that. His wife, Ellen, was deficient in many respects, and resented his constructive criticism. She took it personally. They bickered, and she threatened to leave him. Wharton believed that she was having an affair. George, their son, slouched around the house all day and paid no attention when Wharton described all the sports and hobbies that an eleven-year-old boy ought to be interested in.

Wharton dreamed of a place in the country where George would be outside all day, making friends and hiking, and Ellen would have a garden. In his dream Wharton saw her look up and smile as he came toward her.

He sometimes went camping for a few days when things got bad at home. On one of these trips he saw a large piece of land that the government was selling and decided to buy it. The property was heavily wooded, had a small pond surrounded by birch trees, and a good sturdy building. The building needed some work, but Wharton thought that such a project would bring them all together.

When he told Ellen about it she said, "Are you kidding?"

"I've never been more serious," Wharton said. "And it wouldn't hurt you to show a little enthusiasm."

"No way," Ellen said. "Count me out."

Wharton went ahead and arranged the move. He was sure that when the moment came, Ellen would go with them. He never lost this conviction, not even when she got a job and had a lawyer draw up separation papers. But the moment came and went, and finally Wharton and George left without her.

They had been on the land for almost a year when Wharton began to hear shots from beyond the meadow. The shooting woke him at dawn and disturbed him at his work, and he couldn't make up his mind what to do. He hoped that it would just stop. The noise had begun to wake George, and in his obsessive way he would not leave off asking questions about it. Also, though he seldom played there, George had developed a sense of injury at being kept out of the woods. Ellen was coming up for a visit—her first—and she would make a stink.

The shooting continued. It went on for two weeks, three weeks, well past Easter. On the morning of the day Ellen was supposed to arrive Wharton heard two shots, and he knew he had to do something. He decided to go and talk to his neighbor Vernon. Vernon understood these things.

George caught Wharton leaving the house and asked if he could go play with his friend Rory.

"Absolutely not," Wharton said, and headed up the path toward the road. The ground was swollen and spongy with rain. The fenceposts had a black and soggy look, and the ditches on either side of the road were loud with the rushing of water. Wharton dodged mudholes, huffing a little, and contemplated Rory.

To help George make friends during the previous summer Wharton had driven him to a quarry where the local children swam. George splashed around by himself at one end and pretended that he was having a fine old time, as his eyes ticked back and forth to the motion of the other children flying from bank to bank on the rope swing, shouting "Banzai!" when they let go and reached out to the water.

One afternoon Wharton built a fire and produced hot dogs for the children to roast. He asked their names and introduced George. He told them that they should feel free to come and visit George whenever they liked. They could swim in the pond, or play hide-and-seek in the woods. When they had eaten they thanked him and went back to their end of the quarry while George went back to his. Wharton considered rounding them up for a nature walk, but he never got around to it. A few days before the weather turned too cold for swimming George caught a garter snake in the rushes by the bank, and another boy came over to take a look. That night George asked if he could sleep over at Rory's.

"Who's Rory?"

"Just a guy."

Rory eventually came to their house for a reciprocal visit. Wharton did not think that he was an acceptable friend for George. He would not meet Wharton's eye, and had a way of laughing to himself. Rory and George whispered and giggled all night, and a few days later Wharton found several burnt matches in George's room which George would not account for. He hoped that the boy would enlarge his circle of friends when school began, but this never happened. Wharton fretted about George's shyness. Friends were a blessing and he wanted George to have many friends. In Wharton's opinion,

George's timidity was the result of his being underdeveloped physically. Wharton advised him to take up weight lifting.

Over the mountains to the east a thin line of clouds was getting thicker. Wharton felt a growing dampness in the air as he turned into his neighbor's gate.

He disliked having to ask Vernon for favors or advice, but at times he had no choice. Twice during the winter his car had slipped off the icy, unbanked road, and both times Vernon had pulled him out. He showed Wharton how to keep the raccoons out of his garbage, and how to use a chain saw. Wharton was grateful, but he suspected that Vernon had begun to think of himself as his superior.

He found Vernon in the yard, loading five-gallon cans into the back of his truck. This pleased Wharton. He would not have to go into the dirty, evil-smelling house. Vernon had rented most of the place out to a commune from Seattle, and Wharton was appalled at their sloth and resolute good cheer. He was further relieved not to have to go inside because he wished to avoid one of the women. They had kept company for a short, unhappy time during the winter; the situation was complicated, and Wharton already had enough to keep him busy for the day.

"Well, howdy there," Vernon said. "And how's every little thing down at the lower forty?"

Wharton noticed that Vernon always countrified his speech when he was around. He guessed that Vernon did it to make him feel like a city slicker. Wharton had heard him talk to other people and he sounded normal enough. "Not so good," he said, and lifted one of the cans.

Vernon took it from him very firmly and slid it down the bed of the truck. "You got to use your back hoisting these things," he said. He slammed the tailgate shut and yanked the chain through the slots. The links rattled like bolts in a can.

He took a rag out of his back pocket and blew his nose. "What's the trouble?"

"Someone's been shooting on my land."

"What do you mean, shooting? Shooting what?"

"I don't know. Deer, I suppose."

Vernon shook his head. "Deer have all headed back into the high country by now."

"Well, whatever. Squirrels. Rabbits. The point is that someone has been hunting in the woods without asking my permission."

"It isn't any of us," Vernon said. "I can tell you that much. There's only one rifle in this house and nobody goes near it but me. I wouldn't trust that load of fruitcakes with an empty water pistol."

"I didn't think it was you. It just occurred to me that you might have some idea who it could be. You know the people around here."

Vernon creased his brow and narrowed his eyes to show, Wharton supposed, that he was thinking. "There's one person," he said finally. "You know Jeff Gill from up the road?"

Wharton shook his head.

"I guess you wouldn't have met him at that. He keeps to himself. He's pretty crazy, Jeff Gill. You know that song 'I'm My Own Grandpaw'? Well, Jeff Gill is his own uncle. The Gills," he said, "are a right close family. You want me to call down there, see what's going on?"

"I would appreciate that."

Wharton waited outside, leaning against an empty watering trough. The breeze rippled puddles and blew scraps of paper across the yard. Somewhere a door creaked open and shut. He tried to count the antlers on the front of the barn but gave up. There were over a hundred pairs of them, bleached and silvered by the sun. It was a wonder there were any deer left in the province. Over the front door of the house there were more antlers, and on the porch a set of suitcases and a steamer trunk. Apparently someone was leaving the commune. If so, it would not be the first defection.

Vernon's tenants had had a pretty awful winter. Factions developed over the issues of child care and discipline, sleeping arrangements, cooking, shoveling snow, and the careless use of someone's Deutsche Grammophon records. According to Wharton's lady friend, Vernon had caused a lot of trouble. He made fun of the ideals of the commune with respect to politics, agriculture, religion, and diet, and would not keep his hands off the women. It got to where they were afraid to go out to the woodshed by themselves. Also, he insisted on calling them Hare Krishnas, which they were not.

Wharton's friend wanted to know why, if Vernon couldn't be more supportive of the commune, he had rented the house to them in the first place? And if he hated them so much how come he stayed on in the master bedroom?

Wharton knew the answer to the first question and could guess the answer to the second. Vernon's father had been a wild man and died owing twelve years' back taxes. Vernon needed money. Wharton imagined that he stayed on himself because he had grown up in the house and could not imagine living anywhere else.

Vernon came back into the yard carrying a rifle. Wharton could smell the oil from ten feet away. "I couldn't get anybody down at the Gills'," Vernon said. "Phone's been disconnected. I talked to a guy I knew who works with Jeff, and he says Jeff hasn't been at the mill in over a month. Thinks he's went somewhere else." Vernon held out the rifle. "You know how to work this?"

"Yes," Wharton said.

"Why don't you keep it around for a while. Just till things get sorted out."

Wharton did not want the rifle. As he had told George when George asked for a B-B gun, he believed that firearms were a sign of weakness. He reached out and took the thing, but only because Vernon would feel slighted if he refused it.

"Wow," George said when he saw the rifle. "Are you going to shoot the sniper?"

"I'm not going to shoot anybody," Wharton said. "And I've told you before, the word is poacher, not sniper."

"Yeah, poacher. Where did you get the gun?"

Wharton looked down at his son. The boy had been sawing up and nailing together some scrap lumber. He was sweating and his skin had a flush on it. How thin he was! You would think he never fed the boy, when in fact he went out of his way to prepare wholesome meals for him. Wharton had no idea where the food went, unless, as he suspected, George was giving his lunches to Rory. Wharton began to describe to George the difference between a rifle and a gun but George was not interested. He would be perfectly content to use his present vocabulary for the next eighty years.

"When I was your age," he said, "I enjoyed acquiring new words and learning to use them correctly."

"I know, I know," George said, then mumbled something under his breath.

"What was that?"

"Nothing."

"You said something. Now what did you say?"

George sighed. "'Jeez.'"

Wharton was going to point out that if George wished to

curse he should do so forthrightly, manfully, but he stopped himself. George was not a man, he was a boy, and boys should not be hounded all the time. They should be encouraged. Wharton nodded at the tangle of lumber and congratulated George on doing something both physical and creative. "What is it?" he asked.

"A lair," George said. "For a wolf."

"I see," Wharton said. "That's good." He nodded again and went inside. As he locked the rifle away—he didn't really know how to work it—Wharton decided that he should let George see his lighter side more often. He was capable of better conversation than reminders that "okay" was not a word, that it was prudent not to spend all one's allowance the same day, or that chairs were for sitting in and floors for walking on. Just the other day the plumber had come in to unclog the kitchen sink and he had laughed at several things Wharton had said.

For the rest of the morning Wharton sketched out episodes for his old bread-and-butter strip. This was about a trapper named Pierre who, in the course of his adventures, passed along bits of homespun philosophy and wilderness lore, such as how to treat frostbite and corns, and how to take bearings so that you would not end up walking in circles. The philosophy was anti-materialist, free-thinking stuff, much like the philosophy of Wharton's father, and over the years it had become obnoxious to him. He was mortally tired of the Trapper and his whole bag of tricks, his smugness and sermonizing and his endless cries of "Mon Dieu!" and "Sacre Bleu!" and "Ze ice, she ees breaking up!" Wharton was more interested in his new strip, *Ulysses*, whose hero was a dog searching for his master in the goldfields of the Yukon. Pierre still paid the bills, though, and Wharton could not afford to pull the plug on him.

There was no shooting from the woods, and Wharton's concentration ran deep. He worked in a reverie, and when he happened to look at his watch he realized that he was supposed to have picked up his wife ten minutes earlier. The station was an hour away.

Ellen kept after Wharton all the way home in her flat, smoky voice. She had old grievances and she listed them, but without anger, as if they bored her: his nagging, his slovenliness, his neglect of her. Oh, she didn't mind waiting around bus stations for an hour now and then. But he *always* kept her waiting. Why? Did he want to humiliate her? Was that it?

"No," Wharton said. "I just lost track of the time." The other charges she had brought against him were true and he did not challenge them.

"If there's one thing I can't stand," Ellen said, "it's this suffering-in-silence, stiff-upper-lip crap."

"I'm sorry," Wharton said.

"I know you are. That doesn't change anything. Oh, look at the little colts and fillies!"

Wharton glanced out the window. "Actually," he said, "those are ponies. Shetlands."

She didn't answer.

It rained hard, then cleared just before they came up the drive to the house. Ellen got out of the car and looked around skeptically. In the distance the mountains were draped with thick coils of cloud, and closer up in the foothills the mist lay among the treetops. Water ran down the trunks of the trees and stood everywhere. Wharton picked up Ellen's bags and walked toward the house, naming wildflowers along the path.

"I don't know what you're trying to prove," Ellen said, "living out in the middle of no goddam where at all." She saw

George and shouted and waved. He dropped the board he was hammering and ran to meet her. She knelt on the wet grass and hugged him, pinning his arms to his side. He tried to hug back but finally gave up and waited, looking over Ellen's shoulder at Wharton. Wharton picked up his bags again. "I'll be in the house," he said, and continued up the path, his boots making a sucking noise in the mud.

"House?" Ellen said when she had come inside. "You call this a house? It's a barn or something."

"Actually," Wharton said, "it's a converted stable. The government used to keep mules here."

"I'm all for simple living but God Almighty."

"It's not so bad. We're getting along just fine, aren't we, George?"

"I guess so."

"Why don't you show Mother your room?"

"Okay." George went down the passageway. He waited outside, holding the door like an usher. Ellen looked inside and nodded. "Oh, you set up a cot for me. Thank you, George."

"Dad set it up. I'll sleep there and you can have the bed if you want."

Wharton showed her what was left to see of the house. She hated it. "You don't even have any pictures on the walls!" she said. He admitted that the place lacked warm touches. In the summer he would throw on a coat of paint, maybe buy some curtains. When they came down from the loft where Wharton worked Ellen took a package from her suitcase and gave it to George.

"Well, George," Wharton said, "what do you say?"

"Thank you," George said, not to Ellen but to Wharton.

"Go ahead and open it," Wharton said.

"For Christ's sake," Ellen said.

It was a book, *The World of Wolves*. "Jeez," George said. He sat down on the floor and began thumbing through the pictures.

How could Ellen have guessed at George's interest in wolves? She had an instinct for gifts the way other people had an instinct for finding the right words to say. The world of things was not alien and distasteful to her as it was to Wharton. He despised his possessions with some ostentation; those who gave him gifts went away feeling as if they'd made Wharton party to a crime. He knew that over the years he had caused Ellen to be shy of her own generosity.

"Why don't you read in your bedroom, George? The light here is terrible."

"He can stay," Ellen said.

"Okay," George said, and went down the hall, not lifting his eyes from the page.

"That wasn't as expensive as it looks," Ellen said.

"It was a fine gift," Wharton said. "Wolves are one of George's obsessions these days."

"I got it for a song," Ellen said. She put a cigarette in her mouth and began to rummage through her purse. Finally she turned her bag upside down and dumped it all over the floor. She poked through the contents, then looked up. "Have you got a match?"

"No. You'll have to light it from the stove."

"I suppose you've quit." She said this as though it were an accusation.

"I still enjoy one every now and then," Wharton said.

"Did you read what that doctor said who did the postmortem on Howard Hughes?" asked Ellen, returning from the kitchen. "He said, 'Howard Hughes had lungs just like a baby.' I almost cried when I read that, it made me so nostalgic for when I was young. I'd hate to think what my lungs look like, not to mention my liver and God knows what else." She blew out some smoke and watched it bitterly as it twisted through a slant of light.

"Howard Hughes never let anyone touch him or come close to him," Wharton said. "That's not your style."

"What do you mean by that?"

"Only that there's always a certain risk when we get close—"

"You didn't mean that. You think I've got this big love life going. What a laugh."

"Well, you did."

"I don't want to get into that," Ellen said. "Let's just say I like to be appreciated."

"I appreciated you."

"No. You thought you were too good for me."

Wharton denied this without heat. During most of their marriage he *had* imagined that he was too good for Ellen. He had been wrong about that and now look at the mess he had made. He stood abruptly, but once he was on his feet he could not think of anything to do, so he sat again.

"What's the point, anyway?" Ellen asked, waving her hand around. "Living in a stable, for God's sake, wearing those boots and that dumb hat."

"I was wearing the boots because the ground is muddy and the hat because my head gets cold."

"Who are you trying to kid? You wear the hat because you think it makes you look like Pierre the Trapper. Ees true, no?"

"You've made your point, Ellen. You don't like the house and you don't like me. Actually, I'm not even sure why you came."

"Actually," she said, "I came to see my son."

"I don't understand why you couldn't wait until June. That's only two more months and you'll have him all summer. According to the terms—"

Ellen snorted. "According to the terms," she said. "Come off it."

"Let me finish. I don't have to grant you visiting privileges. This is a courtesy visit. Now if you can't stop finding fault with everything you can leave, and the sooner the better."

"I'll leave tomorrow," Ellen said.

"Suit yourself."

Ellen bent suddenly in her chair. Piece by piece, she picked up the things she'd emptied onto the floor and replaced them in her purse. Then she stood and walked down the passageway to George's room, moving with dignity as if concealing drunkenness, or a limp.

At dinner George announced his intention to acquire a pet wolf. Wharton had entertained a similar fancy at George's age, and the smile he gave his son was addressed to the folly of both their imaginations. George took it as encouragement and pressed on. There was, he said, a man in Sinclair who had two breeding pairs of timber wolves. George knew for sure that a litter was expected any day now.

Wharton wanted to let George down lightly. "They're probably not real wolves," he said. "More likely they're German shepherds, or huskies, or a mix."

"These are real wolves all right," George said.

"How can you be sure?" Ellen asked. "Have you seen them?"

"No, but Rory has."

"Who is Rory?"

"Rory is an acquaintance of George's," Wharton said, "and Rory does not have the last word on every subject, at least not in this house."

"Rory is my friend," George said.

"All right," Wharton said, "I'm willing to accept Rory's testimony that those are real wolves. What I will not accept is the idea of bringing a wild animal into the house."

"They're not wild. Rory says—"

"Rory again!"

"—Rory says that they're just as tame as dogs, only smarter."

"George, be reasonable. A wolf is a killing machine. It needs to kill in order to survive. There's nothing wrong with that, but a wolf belongs in the wild, not on a chain or locked up in a cage somewhere."

"I wouldn't lock him up. He'd have a lair."

"A lair? Is that what you're building?"

George nodded. "I told you."

"George," Ellen said, "why don't you think about a nice dog? Wolves really are very dangerous animals."

George did not want a nice dog. He was willing to admit that wolves were dangerous, but only to the enemies of their friends. This carried him to his last argument, which he played like a trump: a wolf was just exactly what they needed to help them get rid of the sniper.

"Sniper?" Ellen said. "What sniper?"

"He means poacher," Wharton said. "George, I'm at the end of my patience. A wolf belongs with other wolves, not with people. I don't approve of this habit of turning wild animals into pets. Now please drop the subject. And stop playing with your food."

"What poacher?" Ellen asked.

"I'm not hungry," George said.

"Then leave the table."

George went to his room and slammed the door.

"What poacher?"

"Someone has been doing some shooting on the property. It's nothing serious."

"There's someone running around out there with a gun and you say it isn't serious?"

"This used to be public land. I want people to feel like they can use it."

"But this is your home!"

"Ellen—"

"What have you done about it? You haven't done anything at all, have you?"

"No," Wharton said, and got up and left the room. On his way outside he stopped to talk to George. The boy was sitting on the floor, sorting through some junk he kept in a cigar box. "Son," Wharton said, "I'm sorry if I was short with you at dinner."

"It's okay," George said.

"I'm not just being mean," Wharton said. "A mature wolf can weigh over a hundred and fifty pounds. Think what would happen if it turned on you."

"He wouldn't turn on me. He would protect me." George shook the box. "He would love me."

Wharton had intended to go for a walk but decided it was too slippery underfoot. He sat on the front steps instead, hunched down in his coat. The moon was racing through filmy clouds, melting at the edges. The wind had picked up considerably, and Wharton could hear trees creaking in the woods beyond. Gradually the sky lowered and it began to rain. Ellen came out and told Wharton that he had a phone call.

It was the woman from the commune. She was going to be leaving the next day and wanted to come up to say good-bye. Wharton told her that this was not possible just now. The woman was obviously hurt. She had once accused Wharton of not valuing her as a person and he wanted to show that this was not true. "Look," he said, "let me take you to the station to-morrow."

"Forget it."

Wharton insisted and finally she agreed. Only after he hung up did Wharton realize that he might have Ellen along as well. There was just one bus out on Sunday.

Ellen and George were lying on the floor, reading the book together. Ellen patted the place beside her. "Join us?" Wharton shook his head. They were getting on fine without him; he had no wish to break up such a cozy picture. Anyway it would hardly be appropriate for him to go flopping all over the floor after scolding George for the same thing. Still restless, he went up to the loft and worked. It was very late when he finished. He took off his boots at the foot of the ladder and moved as quietly as he could past George's bedroom. When he turned on the light in his own room he saw that Ellen was in his bed. She covered her eyes with her forearm. The soft flesh at the base of her throat fluttered gently with her breathing.

"Did you really want me to stay with George?"

"No," Wharton said. He dropped his clothes on top of the chest that served as dresser and chair. Ellen drew the covers back for him and he slid in beside her.

"Who was that on the phone?" she asked. "Have you got a little something going?"

"We saw each other a few times. The lady is leaving tomorrow."

"I'm sorry. I hate to think of you all alone out here."

Wharton almost said, "Then stay!" but he caught himself.

"There's something I've got to tell you," Ellen said, raising herself on an elbow. "Jesus, what a look."

"What have you got to tell me?"

"It isn't what you're thinking."

"You don't know what I'm thinking."

"The hell I don't." She sank back onto her side. "I'm leaving Vancouver," she said. "I'm not going to be able to take George this summer. That's why I wanted to see him now."

Ellen explained that she did not feel comfortable living alone in the city. She hated her job and the apartment was too small. She was going back to Victoria to see if she couldn't find something better there. She hated to let George down, but this was a bad time for her.

"Victoria? Why Victoria?" Ellen had never spoken well of the place. According to her the people were all stuffed shirts and there was nothing to do there. Wharton could not understand her and said so.

"Right now I need to be someplace I feel at home." That brought Ellen to another point. She was going to need money for travel and to keep body and soul together until she found another job.

"Whatever I can do," Wharton said.

"I knew you'd help."

"I guess this means you don't have to go back tomorrow."

"No. I guess not."

"Why don't you stay for a week? It would mean a lot to George."

"We'll see."

Wharton turned off the light, but he could not sleep for the longest time. Neither could Ellen; she kept turning and arranging herself. Wharton wanted to reach out to her but he wouldn't have felt right about it, so soon after lending her money.

George woke them in the morning. He sat on the edge of the bed, pale and trembling.

"What's wrong, sweetie?" Ellen asked, and then they heard a shot from the woods. She looked at Wharton. Wharton got out of bed, dressed quickly, and went outside.

He knew it was Jeff Gill, had known so the moment he heard the man's name. It sounded familiar, as things to come often did. He even knew what Jeff Gill would look like: short and wiry, with yellow teeth and close-set, porcine eyes. He did not know why Jeff Gill hated him but he surely did, and Wharton felt that in some way the hatred was justified.

It was raining, not hard but drearily. The air had a chill on it and as he circled the house Wharton walked into the mist of his own breathing. Two swallows skimmed the meadow behind the house, dipping and wheeling through the high grass. They did not break their pattern as he walked by them, yellow rubber boots glistening, and passed into the shadow of the tall trees.

He realized that he had not been in these woods for almost a month. He had been afraid to walk on his own land. He still was. "Go away!" he shouted, walking among the straight wet trunks of trees: "Go away!"

There were still clumps of snow lying everywhere, gray and crystalline and impacted with brown needles. The branches of pine and fir and spruce were tipped with sweet new growth. Stirred by the rain, the soil gave off an acid smell, like a compost heap. Wharton stepped under a sugar pine to catch his breath and scrape some of the mud off his boots. They were so heavy he could hardly lift them.

He heard another shot; it came from the direction of the pond and seemed to crash beside him. "Listen!" Wharton yelled. "I've got a rifle too and I'll use it! Go away!" Wharton thought that he was capable of doing what he said, if he had brought the weapon and had known how to work it. He had felt foolish and afraid for so long that he was becoming dangerous.

He walked toward the pond. The banks were ringed with silver birches and he leaned against one of these. The brown water bristled with splashing raindrops. He caught a motion on the surface of the pond, a rippling triangle like an arrowhead with a dark spot at its point. Wharton assumed that it was a duck and stepped out on a small jetty to get a better look.

Suddenly the creature raised its head and stared at Wharton. It was a beaver, swimming on its back. Its gaze was level and unblinking. Its short front legs were folded over its gently rounded belly, reminding Wharton of a Hogarth engraving of an English clubman after a meal. The beaver lowered its head into the pond and then its belly disappeared and its paddle-like tail swung in a wide arc and cracked flat against the surface of the water. The birches around the pond squeezed the sound and made it sharp and loud, like a rifle going off.

Wharton turned and went back to the house and explained everything to Ellen and George. He made breakfast while they dressed, and afterward they all walked down to the pond to look at the beaver. Along the way Wharton slipped and fell and when he tried to stand he fell again. The mud was on his face and even in his hair. Ellen told him that he ought to take a roll in the mud every day, that it would be the making of him.

George reached the bank first and shouted, "I see him! I see him!"

The beaver was old and out of place. A younger beaver had driven him away from his lodge, and during the thaw he had followed a seasonal stream, now gone dry, up to the pond.

When Vernon heard about the beaver he took his rifle back and went to the pond and shot him. Wharton was outraged, but Vernon insisted that the animal would have destroyed the birches and fouled the bottom of the pond, killing the plants and turning the water stagnant. George's biology teacher agreed.

Ellen left at the end of the week. She and Wharton wrote letters, and sometimes, late at night, she called him. They had good talks but they never lived together again. A few days after she left, George's friend Rory turned on him and threw his books and one of his shoes out the schoolbus window, with the help of another boy more to his liking.

But Wharton, standing in the warm rain with his family that morning, did not know that these things would come to pass. Nor did he know that the dog Ulysses would someday free him from the odious Trapper Pierre, or that George would soon—too soon—put on muscle and learn to take care of himself. The wind raised small waves and sent them slapping up against the jetty, so that it appeared to be sliding forward like the hull of a boat. Out in the pond the beaver dove and surfaced again. It seemed to Wharton, watching him move in wide circles upon the water, that the creature had been sent to them, that they had been offered an olive branch and were not far from home.

The Liar

⚜

My mother read everything except books. Advertisements on buses, entire menus as we ate, billboards; if it had no cover it interested her. So when she found a letter in my drawer that was not addressed to her she read it. "What difference does it make if James has nothing to hide?"—that was her thought. She stuffed the letter in the drawer when she finished it and walked from room to room in the big empty house, talking to herself. She took the letter out and read it again to get the facts straight. Then, without putting on her coat or locking the door, she went down the steps and headed for the church at the end of the street. No matter how angry and confused she might be, she always went to four o'clock Mass and now it was four o'clock.

It was a fine day, blue and cold and still, but Mother walked as though into a strong wind, bent forward at the waist with her feet hurrying behind in short, busy steps. My brother and sisters and I considered this walk of hers funny and we smirked at one another when she crossed in front of us to stir the fire, or water a plant. We didn't let her catch us at it. It would have puzzled her to think that there might be anything amusing about her. Her one concession to the fact of humor was an insincere, startling laugh. Strangers often stared at her.

While Mother waited for the priest, who was late, she prayed. She prayed in a familiar, orderly, firm way: first for her late husband, my father, then for her parents—also dead. She said a quick prayer for my father's parents (just touching base; she had disliked them) and finally for her children in order of their ages, ending with me. Mother did not consider originality a virtue and until my name came up her prayers were exactly the same as on any other day.

But when she came to me she spoke up boldly. "I thought he wasn't going to do it anymore. Murphy said he was cured. What am I supposed to do now?" There was reproach in her tone. Mother put great hope in her notion that I was cured. She regarded my cure as an answer to her prayers and by way of thanksgiving sent a lot of money to the Thomasite Indian Mission, money she had been saving for a trip to Rome. She felt cheated and she let her feelings be known. When the priest came in Mother slid back on the seat and followed the Mass with concentration. After communion she began to worry again and went straight home without stopping to talk to Frances, the woman who always cornered Mother after Mass to tell about the awful things done to her by Communists, devil-worshipers, and Rosicrucians. Frances watched her go with narrowed eyes.

Once in the house, Mother took the letter from my drawer and brought it into the kitchen. She held it over the stove with her fingernails, looking away so that she would not be drawn into it again, and set it on fire. When it began to burn her fingers she dropped it in the sink and watched it blacken and flutter and close upon itself like a fist. Then she washed it down the drain and called Dr. Murphy.

The letter was to my friend Ralphy in Arizona. He used to live across the street from us but he had moved. Most of the letter was about a tour we, the junior class, had taken of Alcatraz. That was all right. What got Mother was the last paragraph where I said that she had been coughing up blood and the doctors weren't sure what was wrong with her, but that we were hoping for the best.

This wasn't true. Mother took pride in her physical condition, considered herself a horse: "I'm a regular horse," she would reply when people asked about her health. For several years now I had been saying unpleasant things that weren't true and this habit of mine irked Mother greatly, enough to persuade her to send me to Dr. Murphy, in whose office I was sitting when she burned the letter. Dr. Murphy was our family physician and had no training in psychoanalysis but he took an interest in "things of the mind," as he put it. He had treated me for appendicitis and tonsillitis and Mother thought that he could put the truth into me as easily as he took things out of me, a hope Dr. Murphy did not share. He was basically interested in getting me to understand what I did, and lately he had been moving toward the conclusion that I understood what I did as well as I ever would.

Dr. Murphy listened to Mother's account of the letter, and what she had done with it. He was curious about the wording I had used and became irritated when Mother told him she had burned it. "The point is," she said, "he was supposed to be cured and he's not."

"Margaret, I never said he was cured."

"You certainly did. Why else would I have sent over a thousand dollars to the Thomasite Mission?"

"I said that he was responsible. That means that James

knows what he's doing, not that he's going to stop doing it."

"I'm sure you said he was cured."

"Never. To say that someone is cured you have to know what health is. With this kind of thing that's impossible. What do you mean by curing James, anyway?"

"You know."

"Tell me anyway."

"Getting him back to reality, what else?"

"Whose reality? Mine or yours?"

"Murphy, what are you talking about? James isn't crazy, he's a liar."

"Well, you have a point there."

"What am I going to do with him?"

"I don't think there's much you can do. Be patient."

"I've been patient."

"If I were you, Margaret, I wouldn't make too much of this. James doesn't steal, does he?"

"Of course not."

"Or beat people up or talk back."

"No."

"Then you have a lot to be thankful for."

"I don't think I can take any more of it. That business about leukemia last summer. And now this."

"Eventually he'll outgrow it, I think."

"Murphy, he's sixteen years old. What if he doesn't outgrow it? What if he just gets better at it?"

Finally Mother saw that she wasn't going to get any satisfaction from Dr. Murphy, who kept reminding her of her blessings. She said something cutting to him and he said something pompous back and she hung up. Dr. Murphy stared at the receiver. "Hello," he said, then replaced it on the cradle. He ran his hand over his head, a habit remaining from a time when he had hair. To show that he was a good sport he often joked about his baldness, but I had the feeling that he regretted it deeply. Looking at me across the desk, he must have wished that he hadn't taken me on. Treating a friend's child was like investing a friend's money.

"I don't have to tell you who that was."

I nodded.

Dr. Murphy pushed his chair back and swiveled it around so he could look out the window behind him, which took up most of the wall. There were still a few sailboats out on the Bay, but they were all making for shore. A woolly gray fog had covered the bridge and was moving in fast. The water seemed calm from this far up, but when I looked closely I could see white flecks everywhere, so it must have been pretty choppy.

"I'm surprised at you," he said. "Leaving something like that lying around for her to find. If you really have to do these things you could at least be kind and do them discreetly. It's not easy for your mother, what with your father dead and all the others somewhere else."

"I know. I didn't mean for her to find it."

"Well." He tapped his pencil against his teeth. He was not convinced professionally, but personally he may have been. "I think you ought to go home now and straighten things out."

"I guess I'd better."

"Tell your mother I might stop by, either tonight or tomorrow. And James—don't underestimate her."

While my father was alive we usually went to Yosemite for three or four days during the summer. My mother would drive and Father would point out places of interest, meadows where boom towns once stood, hanging trees, rivers that were said to flow upstream at certain times. Or he read to us; he had that grown-ups' idea that children love Dickens and Sir Walter

Scott. The four of us sat in the back seat with our faces com-posed, attentive, while our hands and feet pushed, pinched, stomped, goosed, prodded, dug, and kicked.

One night a bear came into our camp just after dinner. Mother had made a tuna casserole and it must have smelled to him like something worth dying for. He came into the camp while we were sitting around the fire and stood swaying back and forth. My brother Michael saw him first and elbowed me, then my sisters saw him and screamed. Mother and Father had their backs to him but Mother must have guessed what it was because she immediately said, "Don't scream like that. You might frighten him and there's no telling what he'll do. We'll just sing and he'll go away."

We sang "Row Row Row Your Boat" but the bear stayed. He circled us several times, rearing up now and then on his hind legs to stick his nose into the air. By the light of the fire I could see his doglike face and watch the muscles roll under his loose skin like rocks in a sack. We sang harder as he circled us, com-ing closer and closer. "All right," Mother said, "enough's enough." She stood abruptly. The bear stopped moving and watched her. "Beat it," Mother said. The bear sat down and looked from side to side. "Beat it," she said again, and leaned over and picked up a rock.

"Margaret, don't," my father said.

She threw the rock hard and hit the bear in the stomach. Even in the dim light I could see the dust rising from his fur. He grunted and stood to his full height. "See that?" Mother shouted: "He's filthy. Filthy!" One of my sisters giggled. Mother picked up another rock. "Please, Margaret," my father said. Just then the bear turned and shambled away. Mother pitched the rock after him. For the rest of the night he loitered around the camp until he found the tree where we had hung our food. He ate it all. The next day we drove back to the city.

We could have bought more supplies in the valley, but Father wanted to go and would not give in to any argument. On the way home he tried to jolly everyone up by making jokes, but Michael and my sisters ignored him and looked stonily out the windows.

Things were never easy between my mother and me, but I didn't underestimate her. She underestimated me. When I was little she suspected me of delicacy, because I didn't like being thrown into the air, and because when I saw her and the others working themselves up for a roughhouse I found somewhere else to be. When they did drag me in I got hurt, a knee in the lip, a bent finger, a bloody nose, and this too Mother seemed to hold against me, as if I arranged my hurts to get out of playing.

Even things I did well got on her nerves. We all loved puns except Mother, who didn't get them, and next to my father I was the best in the family. My specialty was the Swifty— "'You can bring the prisoner down,' said Tom condescendingly." Father encouraged me to perform at dinner, which must have been a trial for outsiders. Mother wasn't sure what was going on, but she didn't like it.

She suspected me in other ways. I couldn't go to the movies without her examining my pockets to make sure I had enough money to pay for the ticket. When I went away to camp she tore my pack apart in front of all the boys who were waiting in the bus outside the house. I would rather have gone without my sleeping bag and a few changes of underwear, which I had forgotten, than be made such a fool of. Her distrust was the thing that made me forgetful.

And she thought I was cold-hearted because of what happened the day my father died and later at his funeral. I didn't cry at my father's funeral, and showed signs of boredom during the eulogy, fiddling around with the hymnals. Mother put my hands into my lap and I left them there without moving them as though they were things I was holding for someone else. The effect was ironical and she resented it. We had a sort of reconciliation a few days later after I closed my eyes at school and refused to open them. When several teachers and then the principal failed to persuade me to look at them, or at some reward they claimed to be holding, I was handed over to the school nurse, who tried to pry the lids open and scratched one of them badly. My eye swelled up and I went rigid. The principal panicked and called Mother, who fetched me home. I wouldn't talk to her, or open my eyes, or bend, and they had to lay me on the back seat and when we reached the house Mother had to lift me up the steps one at a time. Then she put me on the couch and played the piano to me all afternoon. Finally I opened my eyes. We hugged each other and I wept. Mother did not really believe my tears, but she was willing to accept them because I had staged them for her benefit.

My lying separated us, too, and the fact that my promises not to lie anymore seemed to mean nothing to me. Often my lies came back to her in embarrassing ways, people stopping her in the street and saying how sorry they were to hear that _____ . No one in the neighborhood enjoyed embarrassing Mother, and these situations stopped occurring once everybody got wise to me. There was no saving her from strangers, though. The summer after Father died I visited my uncle in Redding and when I got back I found to my surprise that Mother had come to meet my bus. I tried to slip away from the gentleman who had sat next to me but I couldn't shake him. When he saw Mother embrace me he came up and presented her with a card and told her to get in touch with him if things got any worse. She gave him his card back and told him to mind his own business. Later, on the way home, she made me repeat what I had said to the man. She shook her head. "It's not fair to people," she said, "telling them things like that. It confuses them." It seemed to me that Mother had confused the man, not I, but I didn't say so. I agreed with her that I shouldn't say such things and promised not to do it again, a promise I broke three hours later in conversation with a woman in the park.

It wasn't only the lies that disturbed Mother; it was their morbidity. This was the real issue between us, as it had been between her and my father. Mother did volunteer work at Children's Hospital and St. Anthony's Dining Hall, collected things for the St. Vincent de Paul Society. She was a lighter of candles. My brother and sisters took after her in this way. My father was a curser of the dark. And he loved to curse the dark. He was never more alive than when he was indignant about something. For this reason the most important act of the day for him was the reading of the evening paper.

Ours was a terrible paper, indifferent to the city that bought it, indifferent to medical discoveries—except for new kinds of gases that made your hands fall off when you sneezed—and indifferent to politics and art. Its business was outrage, horror, gruesome coincidence. When my father sat down in the living room with the paper Mother stayed in the kitchen and kept the children busy, all except me, because I was quiet and could be trusted to amuse myself. I amused myself by watching my father.

He sat with his knees spread, leaning forward, his eyes only inches from the print. As he read he nodded to himself. Sometimes he swore and threw the paper down and paced the room, then picked it up and began again. Over a period of time he developed the habit of reading aloud to me. He always started with the society section, which he called the parasite page. This column began to take on the character of a comic strip or a serial, with the same people showing up from one day to the next, blinking in chiffon, awkwardly holding their drinks for the sake of Peninsula orphans, grinning under sunglasses on the deck of a ski hut in the Sierras. The skiers really got his goat, probably because he couldn't understand them. The activity itself was inconceivable to him. When my sisters went to Lake Tahoe one winter weekend with some friends and came back excited about the beauty of the place, Father calmed them right down. "Snow," he said, "is overrated."

Then the news, or what passed in the paper for news: bodies unearthed in Scotland, former Nazis winning elections, rare animals slaughtered, misers expiring naked in freezing houses upon mattresses stuffed with thousands, millions; marrying priests, divorcing actresses, high-rolling oilmen building fantastic mausoleums in honor of a favorite horse, cannibalism. Through all this my father waded with a fixed and weary smile.

Mother encouraged him to take up causes, to join groups, but he would not. He was uncomfortable with people outside the family. He and my mother rarely went out, and rarely had people in, except on feast days and national holidays. Their guests were always the same, Dr. Murphy and his wife and several others whom they had known since childhood. Most of these people never saw each other outside our house and they didn't have much fun together. Father discharged his obligations as host by teasing everyone about stupid things they had said or done in the past and forcing them to laugh at themselves.

Though Father did not drink, he insisted on mixing cocktails for the guests. He would not serve straight drinks like rum-and-Coke or even Scotch-on-the-rocks, only drinks of his own devising. He gave them lawyerly names like "The Advocate," "The Hanging Judge," "The Ambulance Chaser," "The Mouthpiece," and described their concoction in detail. He told long, complicated stories in a near-whisper, making everyone lean in his direction, and repeated important lines; he also repeated the important lines in the stories my mother told, and corrected her when she got something wrong. When the guests came to the ends of their own stories he would point out the morals.

Dr. Murphy had several theories about Father, which he used to test on me in the course of our meetings. Dr. Murphy had by this time given up his glasses for contact lenses, and lost weight in the course of fasts which he undertook regularly. Even with his baldness he looked years younger than when he had come to the parties at our house. Certainly he did not look like my father's contemporary, which he was.

One of Dr. Murphy's theories was that Father had exhibited a classic trait of people who had been gifted children by taking an undemanding position in an uninteresting firm. "He was afraid of finding his limits," Dr. Murphy told me: "As long as he kept stamping papers and making out wills he could go on believing that he didn't *have* limits." Dr. Murphy's fascination with Father made me uneasy, and I felt traitorous listening to him. While he lived, my father would never have submitted himself for analysis; it seemed a betrayal to put him on the couch now that he was dead.

I did enjoy Dr. Murphy's recollections of Father as a child. He told me about something that happened when they were in the Boy Scouts. Their troop had been on a long hike and Father had fallen behind. Dr. Murphy and the others decided to ambush him as he came down the trail. They hid in the woods on each side and waited. But when Father walked into the trap none of them moved or made a sound and he strolled on without even knowing they were there. "He had the sweetest look on his face," Dr. Murphy said, "listening to the birds, smelling the flowers, just like Ferdinand the Bull." He also told me that my father's drinks tasted like medicine.

While I rode my bicycle home from Dr. Murphy's office Mother fretted. She felt terribly alone but she didn't call anyone because she also felt like a failure. My lying had that effect on her. She took it personally. At such times she did not think of my sisters, one happily married, the other doing brilliantly at Fordham. She did not think of my brother Michael, who had given up college to work with runaway children in Los Angeles. She thought of me. She thought that she had made a mess of her family.

Actually she managed the family well. While my father was dying upstairs she pulled us together. She made lists of chores and gave each of us a fair allowance. Bedtimes were adjusted and she stuck by them. She set regular hours for homework. Each child was made responsible for the next eldest, and I was given a dog. She told us frequently, predictably, that she loved us. At dinner we were each expected to contribute something, and after dinner she played the piano and tried to teach us to sing in harmony, which I could not do. Mother, who was an admirer of the Trapp family, considered this a character defect.

Our life together was more orderly, healthy, while Father was dying than it had been before. He had set us rules to follow, not much different really than the ones Mother gave us after he got sick, but he had administered them in a fickle way. Though we were supposed to get an allowance we always had to ask him for it and then he would give us too much because he enjoyed seeming magnanimous. Sometimes he punished us for no reason, because he was in a bad mood. He was apt to decide, as one of my sisters was going out to a dance, that she had better stay home and do something to improve herself. Or he would sweep us all up on a Wednesday night and take us ice-skating.

He changed after he learned about the cancer, and became more calm as the disease spread. He relaxed his teasing way with us, and from time to time it was possible to have a conversation with him which was not about the last thing that had made him angry. He stopped reading the paper and spent time at the window.

He and I became close. He taught me to play poker and sometimes helped me with my homework. But it wasn't his illness that drew us together. The reserve between us had begun to break down after the incident with the bear, during the drive home. Michael and my sisters were furious with him for making us leave early and wouldn't talk to him or look at him. He joked: though it had been a grisly experience we should grin and bear it—and so on. His joking seemed perverse to the others, but not to me. I had seen how terrified he was when the bear came into the camp. He had held himself so still that he had begun to tremble. When Mother started pitching rocks I thought he was going to bolt, really. I understood—I had been frightened too. The others took it as a lark after they got used to having the bear around, but for Father and me it got worse through the night. I was glad to be out of there, grateful to Father for getting me out. I saw that his jokes were how he held himself together. So I reached out to him with a joke: "'There's a bear outside, said Tom intently.'" The others turned cold looks on me. They thought I was sucking up. But Father smiled.

When I thought of other boys being close to their fathers I thought of them hunting together, tossing a ball back and forth, making birdhouses in the basement, and having long talks about girls, war, careers. Maybe the reason it took us so long to get close was that I had this idea. It kept getting in the way of what we really had, which was a shared fear.

Toward the end Father slept most of the time and I watched him. From below, sometimes, faintly, I heard Mother playing the piano. Occasionally he nodded off in his chair while I was reading to him; his bathrobe would fall open then, and I would see the long new scar on his stomach, red as blood against his white skin. His ribs all showed and his legs were like cables.

I once read in a biography of a great man that he "died well." I assume the writer meant that he kept his pain to himself, did not set off false alarms, and did not too much inconvenience those who were to stay behind. My father died well. His irritability gave way to something else, something like serenity. In the last days he became tender. It was as though he had been rehearsing the scene, that the anger of his life had been a kind of stage fright. He managed his audience—us—with an old trouper's sense of when to clown and when to stand on his dignity. We were all moved, and admired his courage, as he intended we should. He died downstairs in a shaft of late afternoon sunlight on New Year's Day, while I was reading to him. I was alone in the house and didn't know what to do. His body did not frighten me but immediately and sharply I missed my father. It seemed wrong to leave him sitting up and I tried to carry him upstairs to the bedroom but it was too hard, alone. So I called up my friend Ralphy across the street. When he came over and saw what I wanted him for he started crying but I made him help me anyway. A couple of hours later Mother got home and when I told her that Father was dead she ran upstairs, calling his name. A few minutes later she came back down. "Thank God," she said, "at least he died in bed." This seemed important to her and I didn't tell her otherwise. But that night Ralphy's parents called. They were, they said, shocked at what I had done and so was Mother when she heard the story, shocked and furious. Why? Because I had not told her the truth? Or because she had learned the truth, and could not go on believing that Father had died in bed? I really don't know.

"Mother," I said, coming into the living room, "I'm sorry about the letter. I really am."

She was arranging wood in the fireplace and did not look at me or speak for a moment. Finally she finished and straightened up and brushed her hands. She stepped back and looked at the fire she had laid. "That's all right," she said. "Not bad for a consumptive."

"Mother, I'm sorry."

"Sorry? Sorry you wrote it or sorry I found it?"

"I wasn't going to mail it. It was a sort of joke."

"Ha ha." She took up the whisk broom and swept bits of bark into the fireplace, then closed the drapes and settled on the couch. "Sit down," she said. She crossed her legs. "Listen, do I give you advice all the time?"

"Yes."

"I do?"

I nodded.

"Well, that doesn't make any difference. I'm supposed to. I'm your mother. I'm going to give you some more advice, for your own good. You don't have to make all these things up, James. They'll happen anyway." She picked at the hem of her skirt. "Do you understand what I'm saying?"

"I think so."

"You're cheating yourself, that's what I'm trying to tell you.

When you get to be my age you won't know anything at all about life. All you'll know is what you've made up."

I thought about that. It seemed logical.

She went on. "I think maybe you need to get out of yourself more. Think more about other people."

The doorbell rang.

"Go see who it is," Mother said. "We'll talk about this later."

It was Dr. Murphy. He and Mother made their apologies and she insisted that he stay for dinner. I went to the kitchen to fetch ice for their drinks, and when I returned they were talking about me. I sat on the sofa and listened. Dr. Murphy was telling Mother not to worry. "James is a good boy," he said. "I've been thinking about my oldest, Terry. He's not really dishonest, you know, but he's not really honest either. I can't seem to reach him. At least James isn't furtive."

"No," Mother said, "he's never been furtive."

Dr. Murphy clasped his hands between his knees and stared at them. "Well, that's Terry. Furtive."

Before we sat down to dinner Mother said grace; Dr. Murphy bowed his head and closed his eyes and crossed himself at the end, though he had lost his faith in college. When he told me that, during one of our meetings, in just those words, I had the picture of a raincoat hanging by itself outside a dining hall. He drank a good deal of wine and persistently turned the conversation to the subject of his relationship with Terry. He admitted that he had come to dislike the boy. Then he mentioned several patients of his by name, some of them known to Mother and me, and said that he disliked them too. He used the word "dislike" with relish, like someone on a diet permitting himself a single potato chip. "I don't know what I've done wrong," he said abruptly, and with reference to no particular thing. "Then again maybe I haven't done anything wrong. I don't know what to think anymore. Nobody does."

"I know what to think," Mother said.

"So does the solipsist. How can you prove to a solipsist that he's not creating the rest of us?"

This was one of Dr. Murphy's favorite riddles, and almost any pretext was sufficient for him to trot it out. He was a child with a card trick.

"Send him to bed without dinner," Mother said. "Let him create that."

Dr. Murphy suddenly turned to me. "Why do you do it?" he asked. It was a pure question, it had no object beyond the satisfaction of his curiosity. Mother looked at me and there was the same curiosity in her face.

"I don't know," I said, and that was the truth.

Dr. Murphy nodded, not because he had anticipated my answer but because he accepted it. "Is it fun?"

"No, it's not fun. I can't explain."

"Why is it all so sad?" Mother asked. "Why all the diseases?"

"Maybe," Dr. Murphy said, "sad things are more interesting."

"Not to me," Mother said.

"Not to me, either," I said. "It just comes out that way."

After dinner Dr. Murphy asked Mother to play the piano. He particularly wanted to sing "Come Home Abbie, the Light's on the Stair."

"That old thing," Mother said. She stood and folded her napkin deliberately and we followed her into the living room. Dr. Murphy stood behind her as she warmed up. Then they sang "Come Home Abbie, the Light's on the Stair," and I watched him stare down at Mother intently, as if he were trying to remember something. Her own eyes were closed. After that they sang "O Magnum Mysterium." They sang it in parts and I regretted that I had no voice, it sounded so good.

"Come on, James," Dr. Murphy said as Mother played the last chords. "These old tunes not good enough for you?"

"He just can't sing," Mother said.

When Dr. Murphy left, Mother lit the fire and made more coffee. She slouched down in the big chair, sticking her legs straight out and moving her feet back and forth. "That was fun," she said.

"Did you and Father ever do things like that?"

"A few times, when we were first going out. I don't think he really enjoyed it. He was like you."

I wondered if Mother and Father had had a good marriage. He admired her and liked to look at her; every night at dinner he had us move the candlesticks slightly to right and left of center so he could see her down the length of the table. And every evening when she set the table she put them in the center again. She didn't seem to miss him very much. But I wouldn't really have known if she did, and anyway I didn't miss him all that much myself, not the way I had. Most of the time I thought about other things.

"James?"

I waited.

"I've been thinking that you might like to go down and stay with Michael for a couple of weeks or so."

"What about school?"

"I'll talk to Father McSorley. He won't mind. Maybe this problem will take care of itself if you start thinking about other people."

"I do."

"I mean helping them, like Michael does. You don't have to go if you don't want to."

"It's fine with me. Really. I'd like to see Michael."

"I'm not trying to get rid of you."

"I know."

Mother stretched, then tucked her feet under her. She sipped noisily at her coffee. "What did that word mean that Murphy used? You know the one?"

"Paranoid? That's where somebody thinks everyone is out to get him. Like that woman who always grabs you after Mass—Frances."

"Not paranoid. Everyone knows what that means. Sol-something."

"Oh. Solipsist. A solipsist is someone who thinks he creates everything around him."

Mother nodded and blew on her coffee, then put it down without drinking from it. "I'd rather be paranoid. Do you really think Frances is?"

"Of course. No question about it."

"I mean really *sick*?"

"That's what paranoid *is*, is being sick. What do you think, Mother?"

"What are you so angry about?"

"I'm not angry." I lowered my voice. "I'm not angry. But you don't believe those stories of hers, do you?"

"Well, no, not exactly. I don't think she knows what she's saying, she just wants someone to listen. She probably lives all by herself in some little room. So she's paranoid. Think of that. And I had no idea. James, we should pray for her. Will you remember to do that?"

I nodded. I thought of Mother singing "O Magnum Mysterium," saying grace, praying with easy confidence, and it came to me that her imagination was superior to mine. She could imagine things as coming together, not falling apart. She looked at me and I shrank; I knew exactly what she was going to say. "Son," she said, "do you know how much I love you?"

The next afternoon I took the bus to Los Angeles. I looked forward to the trip, to the monotony of the road and the empty fields by the roadside. Mother walked with me down the long concourse. The station was crowded and oppressive. "Are you sure this is the right bus?" she asked at the loading platform.

"Yes."

"It looks so old."

"Mother—"

"All right." She pulled me against her and kissed me, then held me an extra second to show that her embrace was sincere, not just like everyone else's, never having realized that everyone else does the same thing. I boarded the bus and we waved at each other until it became embarrassing. Then Mother began checking through her handbag for something. When she had finished I stood and adjusted the luggage over my seat. I sat and we smiled at each other, waved when the driver gunned the engine, shrugged when he got up suddenly to count the passengers, waved again when he resumed his seat. As the bus pulled out my mother and I were looking at each other with plain relief.

I had boarded the wrong bus. This one was bound for Los Angeles but not by the express route. We stopped in San Mateo, Palo Alto, San Jose, Castroville. When we left Castroville it began to rain, hard; my window would not close all the way, and a thin stream of water ran down the wall onto my seat. To keep dry I had to stay away from the wall and lean forward. The rain fell harder. The engine of the bus sounded as though it were coming apart.

In Salinas the man sleeping beside me jumped up but before I had a chance to change seats his place was taken by an enormous woman in a print dress, carrying a shopping bag. She took possession of her seat and spilled over onto half of mine, backing me up to the wall. "That's a storm," she said loudly, then turned and looked at me. "Hungry?" Without waiting for an answer she dipped into her bag and pulled out a piece of chicken and thrust it at me. "Hey, by God," she hooted, "look at him go to town on that drumstick!" A few people turned and smiled. I smiled back around the bone and kept at it. I finished that piece and she handed me another, and then another. Then she started handing out chicken to the people in the seats near us.

Outside of San Luis Obispo the noise from the engine grew suddenly louder and just as suddenly there was no noise at all. The driver pulled off to the side of the road and got out, then got on again dripping wet. A few moments later he announced that the bus had broken down and they were sending another bus to pick us up. Someone asked how long that might take and the driver said he had no idea. "Keep your pants on!" shouted the woman next to me. "Anybody in a hurry to get to L.A. ought to have his head examined."

The wind was blowing hard around the bus, driving sheets of rain against the windows on both sides. The bus swayed gently. Outside the light was brown and thick. The woman next to me pumped all the people around us for their itineraries and said whether or not she had ever been where they were from or where they were going. "How about you?" She slapped my knee. "Parents own a chicken ranch? I hope so!" She laughed. I told her I was from San Francisco. "San Francisco, that's where my husband was stationed." She asked me what I did there and I told her I worked with refugees from Tibet.

"Is that right? What do you do with a bunch of Tibetans?"

"Seems like there's plenty of other places they could've gone," said a man in front of us. "Coming across the border like that. We don't go there."

"What do you do with a bunch of Tibetans?" the woman repeated.

"Try to find them jobs, locate housing, listen to their problems."

"You understand that kind of talk?"

"Yes."

"Speak it?"

"Pretty well. I was born and raised in Tibet. My parents were missionaries over there."

Everyone waited.

"They were killed when the Communists took over."

The big woman patted my arm.

"It's all right," I said.

"Why don't you say some of that Tibetan?"

"What would you like to hear?"

"Say 'The cow jumped over the moon.'" She watched me, smiling, and when I finished she looked at the others and shook her head. "That was pretty. Like music. Say some more."

"What?"

"Anything."

They bent toward me. The windows suddenly went blind with rain. The driver had fallen asleep and was snoring gently to the swaying of the bus. Outside the muddy light flickered to pale yellow, and far off there was thunder. The woman next to me leaned back and closed her eyes and then so did all the others as I sang to them in what was surely an ancient and holy tongue.

ABOUT THE AUTHOR

TOBIAS WOLFF grew up in the Pacific Northwest, where many of his stories are set. His fiction has appeared in the *Atlantic, Esquire, Vanity Fair, Antaeus*, and many other magazines and reviews in this country and abroad. Mr. Wolff has received numerous honors and awards, including the 1985 PEN/Faulkner Award for THE BARRACKS THIEF. He lives with his wife, Catherine, and their two sons, in upstate New York, where he teaches at Syracuse University.